Comeuppance Served Cold

COMEUPPANCE SERVED COLD

MARION DEEDS

A TOM DOHERTY ASSOCIATES BOOK

NEW YORK

COMEUPPANCE SERVED COLD

Edited by Emily Goldman

Cover art by Helen Crawford-White
Cover design by Christine Foltzer

A Tordotcom Book
Published by Tom Doherty Associates
120 Broadway
New York, NY 10271

www.tor.com

ISBN 978-1-250-81108-0 (ebook)
ISBN 978-1-250-81107-3 (trade paperback)

First Edition: March 2022

Dedication TK

Author's Note

This book contains instances of patriarchal, racist, and ableist violence, both verbal and physical.

Comeuppance Served Cold

NEAR DAWN, NOVEMBER 17, 1929

SEATTLE, WASHINGTON

SHE PRESSED THE MASK, as light as a silk scarf, against her face. Tiny invisible claws gripped her flesh. Closing her eyes, she pictured the body that would veil her: a tall man with a crown of golden hair. She retrieved her valise from the coat closet and went into the study to make one final check.

The body sprawled on the sofa. Black hair spilled over the woman's white blouse, and her left hand trailed on the floor. One of her worn shoes hung half off her foot. Green eyes, already clouding, stared up at the marquetry ceiling.

The masked woman shut the study doors behind her, and crossed the marble foyer. Outside, she walked down to the sidewalk, where she stood for a moment, waiting. A cook came out of the house across the street, carrying a market basket. Just what she was waiting for. She turned, one hand pressed to her head, and limped steadily north up the street.

"Mr. Earnshaw? Are you all right?" the cook called after her. She ignored it.

She walked for half a block. In the shadow of a neighboring house, she stopped, imagining a stout woman in black, a maid out on a near-dawn errand. Her skin itched as the mask changed its illusion. She walked for three more blocks. The sky began to lighten. Two sedans, one with a gold shield on the door, sped past her, heading down the street. Around the next corner, a black taxi sat waiting. She ducked behind a shrub, took off the mask, and put it into her valise.

"You said an hour," the cabbie said as she climbed in. "You cut it close."

He turned around to look at her, waiting. She lowered the bag of jewelry she'd taken from the vault into a large brown envelope. Her fingers brushed over the small stack of passports tucked into a corner of the valise.

"Where to, miss? The waterfront?"

There was a freighter leaving for Astoria in one hour. In Astoria she could catch the train to Wichita, where her client lived.

"Yes, with a stop first," she said as he pulled out onto Broadway Avenue. "Violet's Hat Shop."

"Miss, that's a speakeasy," he said. "They'll be closed by now."

She smiled. "They'll open for me," she said.

PART ONE

ORPHAN

Chapter One

NOVEMBER 4, 1929
(THIRTEEN DAYS BEFORE)

AMBROSE EARNSHAW, Seattle's Commissioner of Magi, looked over his wide ebony desk at the young woman seated across it. "Mortimer Lester is a good friend," he said, "but he is not a great a judge of character. I *am,* and I investigate thoroughly." He touched the open file folder before him.

The woman nodded. Her expression was serious but not anxious. She was pretty, with green eyes and black hair, unfashionably long, tucked up bob-like under a gray cloche. Her hands were folded, but he could see where a tear in the thumb seam of one glove had been nearly perfectly mended. Her white blouse was impeccably pressed. The gray wool skirt she wore, which ended just below her knee, was not in the latest fashion.

"You came here from California, and you told me you attended Miss Meritage's Young Women's Academy in San Diego," he said.

"My parents died when I was ten, and Uncle John was the only one who could take me in." She had a low-pitched voice. "When I was thirteen, my aunt got sick. With the four boys, they couldn't look after me, so I went to Miss Meritage's."

"I have her letter here." He cleared his throat and read aloud,

"Miss White was a conscientious and obedient student. Even though she possesses no magical affinity, she is a careful and methodical mixer of potions. She is reliable, punctual, and tidy. If the position you are filling does not require great imagination, she will do well. I recommend her to you."

If Miss White was hurt by this blunt assessment, it didn't show.

"You cared for Mortimer's great-aunt, in Tarzana, until she crossed over."

"Yes." Miss White shifted her hands. "I came to Seattle looking for work. Mr. Lester told me you might have a position."

"I do," he said. He glanced around the room, stroking his mustache with thumb and forefinger. His study always filled him with satisfaction, from the teak wainscoting to the marquetry ceiling carved of bird's-eye maple. The rich Persian rugs—chosen by his wife, now five years dead—ran up to the French doors, their thin drapes drawn back to show a view of the flagstone terrace and the autumn garden.

"I've done a bit of research about you too, Mr. Earnshaw," Dolly White said. "I understand you are the Commissioner of Magi, and your eldest child, Francis, is in the Order of Saint Michael the Protector, which I assume is a magical police force. Or part of your commission? I don't completely understand."

"The Order is less formal. Our police force is filled with shortsighted fools, too timorous to take necessary action. There's a need for a volunteer force to pick up the slack."

A puzzled frown wrinkled her forehead. "A vigilance committee?"

"That's an old-fashioned term, Miss White. The Order of Saint Michael merely protects the populace where the police cannot." He shot his cuffs. "As for the Commission, it's a . . . well, a governing council. We recommend policy on magic to the mayor and the city council, and we investigate complaints. We're responsible for the licensing of magical practitioners and the collecting of fees."

"We didn't have those in California, I think," she said.

"California is a hotbed of magical crime."

A silence fell.

"Well," Dolly said, "I admit I'm confused. You wanted a companion for your daughter, but I've seen her picture in the society pages, and she isn't an invalid, is she?"

"My daughter is a drunkard."

Dolly White raised her eyebrows.

"Fiona is about to be engaged to Antonio Arbelio, the scion of a fine magical family. But she, lately . . . in the past six months, she has been frequenting a vile criminal enterprise, a speakeasy run by a loathsome colored woman named Violet Solomon. Fiona's behavior grows wilder and more outrageous each day." He cleared his throat. "We haven't even had the engagement party yet. I've thought of moving up the wedding date, but—"

"Oh, no, you mustn't." Dolly shook her head. "That leaves both families open to the worst kinds of gossip."

"I see you understand. She's gotten wilder and wilder. Last week she drove her car into a light pole. As if I didn't have enough on my mind last week, what with . . . well. Something must be done. The trouble . . . the drinking is even worse, because I believe the gin is spiked with shimmer-shim. That terrible stuff should be outlawed."

"The herb shimmer has a valid use, Mr. Earnshaw, as a pain reliever."

He stared then smiled a bit sourly. "I forgot you were a scholar of potions. Well, once Fiona is safely married, there might be a place for you on the Commission staff. Unless Fiona wants to keep you on. If you can keep her away from the precipice until—"

The doors opened, and his troublesome daughter reeled into the room, wrapped in a pink silk dressing gown. Fluffy pink feathered mules covered her feet. "Are you interviewing my new jailor, Daddy?"

"Don't be flippant. Miss White, my daughter, Fiona."

Ignoring Dolly's outstretched hand, Fiona staggered over to the other chair and fell into it. The diffuse afternoon light from the French doors bleached her wavy blond bob to the color of a dandelion crown. "I hope he's going to pay you plenty, Miss White," she said. She yawned. "You'll need it. Lord! I'm tired."

"How can you be tired? It's two in the afternoon. You've slept through breakfast and lunch."

Dolly leaned forward, staring into the girl's face. "You're under the influence of shimmer-shim right now."

"Good Lord," Earnshaw said.

Fiona smiled and closed her eyes. "Gin and shim, my favorite."

"I can help with this," Dolly said. "We'll try an infusion of Paean's Touch."

Earnshaw tugged the bellpull once. As Fiona struggled to her feet, a young maid came into the room.

"Inez, get Miss White what she needs," Earnshaw said.

"Hot water in a teapot, with honey, please," Dolly said. "And we'll take it in the drawing room."

"I hate tea," Fiona said, "and I *hate* the drawing room."

"Too bad for you, then," Dolly said, taking the girl's arm.

They crossed the marble foyer into the drawing room.

Ambrose Earnshaw waited until they left the room. He opened a small wooden box on his desk. Inside, a green jewel nestled into a nest of gold wire. He touched the stone and prepared to listen.

~

The room's pale silk drapes had been drawn open, giving Dolly a view of the mansion's garden. Fiona winced and covered her eyes.

The maid carried in a tray. Dolly poured a cup of water, added a dollop of golden honey, and dropped in a Paean's Touch sachet from her bag.

"Are you poisoning me?" Fiona's pupils were the pinpricks of someone doped up on shim. "Surely Daddy wouldn't have spent a week checking the bona fides of a poisoner when he could hire one in an hour."

Dolly thought the girl had swallowed a shot of shim within the last hour. Plainly, she had the stuff in the house. "You think this behavior embarrasses your father," she said, "but it just strengthens his position." She handed Fiona the cup. "Here, blow on this. It's hot."

"Aren't you bold behind Daddy's back," Fiona said. The cup rattled slightly on its saucer.

"I'd say it to his face," said Dolly. "Now drink it."

Grumbling, Fiona drank the tea. She set the cup on the tray and dropped back into the chair. "He's impressed you, hasn't he? Seattle's White King of Magic."

"He seems to care about you."

She shook her head. "You don't know anything about my

fam—" She sat up. An expression of surprise crossed her face. "I—I feel . . . awake."

Dolly nodded. "And you can continue to feel awake, and better, as long as you avoid alcohol and shimmer-shim. It'll take about three days for Paean's Touch to drive the shim out of your system."

Fiona pouted. "What if I don't *want* it out of my system?"

"Ask me that question again in four days."

Fiona laughed. "Aren't you clever! I'm hungry. Let's go to the kitchen and get Mrs. Chambers to make us something to eat."

~

Earnshaw monitored the change in his daughter's tone. Miss White seemed to be a good choice. Her references were realistic, not the glowing testimonials he instinctively distrusted. She was poor but not a pushover, and clearly, she had Fiona managed.

He closed the file, pushed it to one side, and reached for some Commission paperwork. An hour later, long strides clapped across the foyer.

"So, is Fiona's duenna here yet?"

Earnshaw looked at his son, Francis, lounging against the doorjamb.

"Her name's Dolly White. She'll be helping Fiona until the wedding is on track. Perhaps she can even assist with the planning. She seems organized."

Francis smiled. "Tony Arbelio can help with the planning too. That little cake-eater could even do the flowers."

Earnshaw stared at his son. Francis gazed back, half smiling.

"Arbelio may disgust me too," Earnshaw said, "but we need this alliance. We need it more than ever since Black Tuesday."

"You do," Francis said, as if agreeing.

"My needs *are* your needs, Francis. I won't clean up after you anymore."

Francis sketched a mocking military salute in his father's direction and turned away from the door.

"Francis? No trouble with this girl. I mean it."

"The poor mouse? Sure, Dad, sure. *Semper Servo*."

~

The cook was a cheerful Irish woman who had married a sailor and ended up in Seattle. She made a cheese sandwich and poured a glass of milk for Fiona and offered Dolly some soup. She was delighted to see Fiona awake and eating.

While Fiona was finishing her sandwich, Inez entered the kitchen to tell Dolly Mr. Earnshaw wanted to see her. She returned to the study. They shook hands on a monthly stipend, and Dolly stood while Earnshaw spoke a long litany of strange-sounding words. "The house has a magical lock as well as physical ones," he said. "It recognizes you now. You will be able to come and go without difficulty."

Inez showed her up to her room. Across the hall from Fiona's, it was about half the size, since it shared a wall with the servants' staircase. Fiona's room was papered in peach-colored wallpaper—an Art Deco depiction of ginkgo leaves—with a large window looking down over the lawn and garden. Pale-pink paint covered Dolly's new walls, and her window was half the size of Fiona's.

Dolly unpacked her valise, which Mr. Earnshaw had sent

Inez to fetch from the boarding house. Her three frocks and two skirts looked lonely in the corner of the armoire. Blouses and underthings barely filled a drawer. She drew off her gloves. Mr. Earnshaw's sharp gaze had certainly noted where she'd mended a ripped seam. Last, she lifted out a knitted doll shaped like a sock. At the top of the wool tube, two knots of green yarn and a red crescent made a simple face. Strands of black yarn tumbled down from the top. The skirt was made of long strips of bright silk and linen. Dolly nestled the doll against her pillow and spent a few minutes writing in a cloth-bound journal using the personal shorthand Miss Meritage had taught her.

That evening, she joined the family for dinner in a small, salmon-colored room with a bay window overlooking the kitchen garden. Earnshaw introduced Francis, his firstborn, a tall man with hair a darker shade of gold than Fiona's. He wore a tan suit with an expensive yellow shirt, topaz cuff links, and a ruby tie tack.

Fiona, who had changed into a pale-blue dress, sat across from her. Earnshaw sat at the head of the table while Francis took the other end. The plates carried a geometric platinum pattern Dolly had seen once at Gump's in San Francisco.

Fiona looked lucid but fragile, a lamb caught between two dogs.

"The Doucettes are having a tea dance at the Vance," Francis said. "A reception for a girl cousin who just came out from Duluth."

"I saw that in the newspaper," Dolly said. "An established Seattle family, isn't that right? Of French descent?"

"Ancestry does not confer respectability," Earnshaw said. "I'm shocked at the Vance. It's a fine, upstanding hotel, or it *used* to be."

"I wonder what they'll serve at the buffet. Raw meat?" Francis speared a piece of roast pork loin. "You look frustrated, Dad," he said.

Earnshaw sipped from his wineglass. "Dealing with the spineless," he said. "I can't get the Commission to investigate Lazlo Penske, down on the waterfront."

"That's serious," Francis said. "We have to take care of him. What's the delay?"

Earnshaw made a gesture with his glass. "Our informant is a fishmonger, and the greengrocer's shop is closer to the end of the pier. That milquetoast Sargent persuaded the other commissioners that our informant's motives are suspect, and there is no other evidence."

"Sargent's the worst, that coward." Francis said. "'Live and let live!' Gah. He's as bad as Cahill used to be." He smiled at Dolly. "You'll have to excuse me, Miss White. I'm used to shoptalk at dinner."

"I wonder how much Sargent lost last week," Fiona said to her plate, "following Daddy's investment advice. Black Tuesday? Isn't that what they're calling it?"

Dolly studied the girl over her water glass. Fiona's defiance wasn't just fueled by shim. "Excuse me," she said. "Who is the greengrocer? I thought you were talking about a magus."

Earnshaw smiled, and Francis laughed outright.

"We're terrible with slang, Miss White," Francis said. "A 'greengrocer' is someone who traffics in potions, elixirs, and magical artifacts. All unlicensed and hot as hell, of course, or most of it, anyway."

"Francis means *illegal,*" Earnshaw said. "Most of these people are criminals."

"And a fishmonger?"

Francis guffawed. "Sells fish!"

Dolly smiled. "I see."

Fiona pushed minted peas around on her plate.

"The Commission will come around," Earnshaw said. "These people can't be left unregulated. Penske may even be using elemental magic."

"The Order should pay Mr. Penske a visit," Francis said.

His father shook his head. "Not necessary. I don't want it to look as if I just go around the Commission whenever I can't get my own way."

"But that *is* what you do," Fiona said.

Earnshaw frowned. "Don't blather, Fiona, about things you don't understand."

"I *do* understand," Fiona muttered, staring at her water glass.

Earnshaw turned to Dolly. "Miss White, have you had a chance to see the sights of our lovely city?"

"I've been here a little over a week, so I've seen very little," Dolly said. "You do have a wonderful city library. I can't wait to get back to it. And I need to return some books."

"Inez can do that for you," Earnshaw said. "If you're ever looking for reading matter, you may use my library, in the study. Have you seen the city's parks?"

"Yes, although I'd never seen Volunteer Park before. I'd never been on Broadway Hill until our interview, Mr. Earnshaw."

"Perhaps you and Fiona can arrange a few outings while you are with us. You'll need an escort, though. The streets of Seattle are not always safe for young women."

"Oh, I carry a capsule of oblivion powder with me wherever I go," Dolly said.

"Oblivion powder is very chancy protection," Earnshaw said.

"Unreliable," Francis said. "Many times, we find the young lady insensible and the assailant escaped."

"That's disappointing," Dolly said.

Fiona mashed her peas.

"Francis might find some time to accompany you," Earnshaw said.

Fiona dropped her fork. It clattered on the pristine porcelain. "Miss White, I must warn you off my brother."

"Fiona!" Francis straightened up. "Honestly! Miss White may be poor. That's no reason to treat her like a gold digger!"

"My warning is for *her*," Fiona said. She looked across the table at Dolly, her eyes shining. "My brother is rough with wom—"

"Stop this venom," Earnshaw said.

She whipped her head around. "Venom, is it, Daddy? How many envelopes full of money have you given out to angry fathers? How many maids have we—"

"That is enough!" He slammed the flat of his hand down on the table. Cutlery rattled, and the red wine in Dolly's glass rippled. "You will leave the table, Fiona. You may join us again when you can be civilized!"

Fiona rose. She folded her napkin—Dolly could see her hands shaking—and placed it next to her plate. She walked around her brother and turned at the door. "Oh, Miss White?" she said. She held her cupped hands out in a loose ball and went "*ffft!*" as she drew them apart, her fingers straightening. "*That's* the Earnshaw fortune," she said, "in case Daddy made any grandiose promises." She walked out of sight.

Francis gave Dolly a shamefaced look. "I know you won't

believe me, Miss White, but that . . . harridan isn't Baby Sister. She's normally the sweetest little thing you'd ever meet."

Dolly pressed her napkin to her lips and set it beside her plate. "The outburst was unpleasant, but it's actually a good sign. Agitation and mood swings are part of the withdrawal process from shimmer-shim. She may not have been habituated to it for as long as we first thought."

Earnshaw folded his hands. He stared at the vacant seat, then he smiled. "Looking on the bright side of things, I see. I owe Mortimer Lester a fine dinner." He stood up. "A change of scene is in order; let's have our coffee in the drawing room."

"Thank you, but I think it's time for Fiona to have another dose of Paean's Touch."

"No, join us. Fiona should have some time to come to her senses."

She followed them out of the dining room. In the short hallway between Mr. Earnshaw's study and the drawing room, a niche held an armless chair upholstered in coral pink, a small table, and a candlestick telephone, an attractive bit of design Dolly thought probably cost a pretty penny. Once they were settled, Inez brought in coffee, cream, and sugar on a tray. She served Earnshaw and Francis then Dolly. When Inez left the room, Dolly took a sip and said, "Will you tell me more about what you do, Mr. Earnshaw, at the Commission of Magi? If it's no trouble."

"We provide instruction for those who become aware of their magical abilities. We administer testing. Mostly, we ensure the citizens of this city are treated fairly and not cheated by the magical practitioners and that they are kept protected."

"It sounds like quite an undertaking."

"It is. There has been a council of magicians of one sort or another in Seattle since 1860, although for too long it was a cabal of the magically powerful, sharing knowledge and skills with each other and turning on weaker magicians. But no longer."

"Some say David Denny himself was a magician," Francis said, smiling, "but that's just an old women's tale."

"David Denny?"

"One of the founders of Seattle."

She gave a quick nod and took another sip of coffee.

"What do you know of magic, Miss White?"

"What every schoolgirl does, I suppose. There are parts of San Diego where I would never go without an amulet or a blessed medal. And I've used black tourmaline to check for spells or illusions. At Miss Meritage's school, she taught some magic to those with ability, but I wasn't one. I learned to mix potions."

"Botanical magic is quite common," Mr. Earnshaw said. He folded one leg over the other, his foot jutting out into the room.

"It is, but I have none. Potion mixing is a matter of accuracy, ratios, careful measurement. Any magic . . . well, *artistry,* really, comes from the knowledge of the quality of the herb, the strength of the essential oil, what flavorings would complement or contrast. Around the edges, I would say, is where one can improvise. It's a bit like—" She had started to say *like jazz* but then changed course. "Like baking."

Francis gave a soft laugh. "But you know the basics about the field."

"Well. I know there is elemental magic and there are some elemental beings, although I don't understand their existence. And I know people have encountered the Twilight Folk."

"We call them the Fair Folk," Francis said.

His father frowned. "They're best avoided."

Dolly dipped her head. "There is plant magic, botanical magic, as you said, word magic, and various illusions. Certainly I've heard of shape-shifters. There were prominent wolf families in San Diego, like the O'Malleys."

"Shape-shifters are humans whose condition is drawn from the earth element," Mr. Earnshaw said. "Sadly, it can affect people from all walks of life. The lowest of the magics, all instinct and no intellect. They are not magicians, really, not much above the animals whose shape they share." He set his cup on the side table, planted both feet on the floor, and leaned forward. "Here's what you must understand, Miss White: Fundamentally, all magic is about vibration. Vibration can be harnessed and controlled. That is the nature of magic."

"I don't understand," Dolly said, leaning forward slightly too.

Out of his father's view, Francis rolled his eyes and took a gulp of coffee.

"The earliest magic, the most primitive and primal, was *chant,* which is a form of vibration. The magic we call *word magic;* spoken blessings, invocations, and curses all spring from that root. What the everyday man going about his business does not realize is this: All things have a vibration, and that vibration can be directed."

She shook her head. "I'm confused. Certainly I can see how a person, an animal, a tree, or a large body of water, a field of growing plants, has a—a rhythm to it, a pulse. But metal? A rock? This escapes me."

"All things give off vibrations. Gold gives off a vibration that melds with many magical ones, making it a fine metal for holding a charm. The vibration of quartz transmits magical energy, for instance. Some gemstones are dense enough to hold magic, even hold elemental energy."

"I've heard of that! A friend at school told me about something called the Firedrake. She said it was—"

"A large ruby holding a trapped fire elemental," Mr. Earnshaw said.

"But word magic is written, isn't it? And protective sigils are drawn. There's no vibration there."

"When you read the words in your mind, your mind gives them the vibration."

Dolly frowned slightly.

Mr. Earnshaw looked at her kindly. "It's very complicated. You needn't worry about understanding it. But you begin to see, with all the complexity, why a commission is needed and why magic must be regulated. It took me years of study, practice, and discipline to become a magus, as opposed to some upstart magician whose power unfolded only last week and has no thought of the consequences. Girls like you must be protected from people like him. Even those who are well-meaning but grew up learning pot magic in their grandmother's kitchen may create a magical disaster simply because they are incapable of understanding the intricacies of what they are doing."

"Yes, I see now." She took another sip.

Mr. Earnshaw, however, wasn't finished. As she drank her cooling coffee, he gave her a history of his studies and how he became a magus. He discussed his inventions and the work he'd done for the government, talking at length about the fine, disciplined, meticulous work needed to trap an air elemental, for instance, and sunder it in order to create a pair of listening gems, which he'd named earshot gems. Dolly nodded.

"Specific ingredients, precise measurements, and steps taken in careful order," she said. "Like baking."

He gave a small smile. "I assure you it's *nothing* like baking, Miss White."

He started to explain further. A yawn built up in her jaw, and she clenched her teeth. Across the room, Francis grinned at her, inviting her to smile with him. She stood and topped off her coffee. Mr. Earnshaw did not let this interrupt him.

Despite all her good intentions, her mind did wander, and when she brought it back to the present, he was saying, "... see why a 'simple herbalist,' who sells healing teas and cooking spices but also mixes up shimmer-shim in a secret room, cannot be ignored. The public must be protected."

She nodded a bit more vigorously than she'd meant to. "It's like Prohibition in a way," she said.

"Prohibition is not efficient. That Solomon woman has been running a criminal enterprise for two years, and the police have done nothing about it. And it's far from the only speakeasy in this town. Prohibition's hardly a model of success. The Commission is far more effective than the government."

She raised her eyebrows in surprise. "Aren't you part of the government? I thought you were part of the city council."

"Oh, no. We work side by side. They could not possibly be in a position of decision-making over *us*."

"I suppose not. They just don't have the expertise."

He smiled approvingly. "That's an intelligent observation, Miss White." How quickly he approved of her wits, she thought, when she agreed with him. "While we provide policy guidance, the city council sets policy and makes laws. A most cumbersome process, and not always satisfactory."

"That must be frustrating." Dolly looked at her wristwatch. She stood up. "Mr. Earnshaw, this has been so valuable, but I must give Fiona her second dose." She set her cup on the tray.

"Of course. We can continue the conversation another time."

She nodded. "Good night," she said. She nodded to Francis also and left the room. Their voices started up immediately, fading as she headed for the kitchen. It took the closing of the kitchen door behind her to silence them completely.

~

She carried up the tray herself. Fiona opened the door to her knock. "I should apologize," she said, "but I'm serious, Dolly. You have to—"

"Calmly, now, Miss Earnshaw," Dolly said. "I've brought you your tea."

Fiona sat by her dressing table and accepted the herbal infusion. "I . . . um, please call me Fiona. May I call you Dolly? And how was your coffee?"

"Of course you may, Fiona. The coffee was excellent. Your father had a lot to tell me, about everything."

"Oh, dear. Was it boring?"

Dolly rolled her eyes and didn't answer.

Fiona sputtered and put her hand over her mouth to stifle her laughter.

They sat quietly while Fiona drank her infusion in methodical swallows.

Dolly said, "The shim is leaving your system, so you may find you have vivid dreams or restlessness and agitation. You may not be able to sleep. You may feel as if your skin is too small for your body. If you wake during the night, if you feel distressed, come knock on my door."

"I see he put you right across the hall," Fiona said. "So I can't sneak out in the small hours and make a run to Violet's."

Dolly nodded silently.

"All right," Fiona said. She looked at Dolly without smiling. "I'll be good."

~

Dolly awoke in the dark. She sat up, pulled on a robe, and walked to the door. Across the hall, she heard whispering and soft thumps, like the closing of dresser drawers.

Behind the door, Fiona was muttering.

Dolly tapped on the door. "Fiona?" She tried the doorknob. It turned easily under her hand.

Fiona stood in the center of the room. She wore a frumpy sweater and wide-legged trousers in some silky fabric. "I can't sleep. I'm twitching. I need . . . a drink. Just one, to help me sleep."

"I'll make some chamomile tea," Dolly said.

A spasm crossed Fiona's face. "I don't need *tea*! I need a real drink! There's a whiskey decanter in Daddy's study. It's vile, but it'll do."

"It *won't* do. It's exactly what you don't need," Dolly said.

Fiona whirled away from her and paced the room. "This isn't worth it. I thought I could—"

Dolly said, "You said four days, remember?"

"Did I? I can't even stand still, I—"

"Then we'll walk around," Dolly said. "You can show me the house."

"In the middle of the night?"

"Physical activity will help calm you." Dolly offered her arm. "Come on. I've seen your father's study, the drawing room, the kitchen, and the breakfast room. Show me the rest."

Fiona flung herself around. "This is what you warned me about, isn't it?"

"This is what I warned you about."

"All right, let me show you the Earnshaw house. We're not on Millionaire's Row, you understand. That was Mama's choice. When her father built them the house as a wedding present, she didn't want to be 'ostentatious.'"

Fiona led her down the stairs, talking the whole way. She showed off the smaller, elegantly decorated parlor and the conservatory, which was cool enough this time of night to make them both shiver. They went back upstairs and turned into the north wing. Her voice dropped to a whisper, but as they walked down the richly carpeted hall, a door opened behind them. Dolly turned. Earnshaw, in a maroon silk dressing gown, looked out at them.

"I'm showing Miss White the house, Daddy," Fiona said. "Being a good hostess."

"At one in the morning?"

"No time like the present."

He looked at Dolly. "This hardly seems appropriate, wandering around after midnight. Fiona should be sleeping, not disrupting the household."

"Mild exercise helps reduce the physical agitation, Mr. Earnshaw."

He eyed them. "Very well. Try not to make too much noise, Fiona. Your brother needs his rest."

"I'll be very quiet," Fiona stage-whispered in a volume that set up buzzing echoes. Dolly took her arm and led her away.

"What's up there?" Dolly asked as the neared the staircase to the third floor.

"Oh. Mostly storage, Daddy's workroom, and his vault."

"You have a vault?"

"Yes. Daddy used to work with jewels, and he has lots of artifacts he's collected or confiscated. Francis does too."

They started up the polished wood steps.

"I thought your father's study was on the first floor, where I met you this morning," Dolly said. "Doesn't he work there?"

"Oh, yes. He and Francis both use the study. But Daddy is a magus, remember."

"I pictured him mostly writing books and scholarly papers, handing down judgments from the Commission, that sort of thing."

Fiona snorted. "Oh, yes, he does all that too. Daddy created some powerful devices during the Great War, though. Remote fire was his best one, but have you heard of earshot gems?"

"He mentioned them tonight. Listening jewels that let us overhear conversations?"

"Yes. Those were Daddy's. They've proved popular after the war too."

"I can imagine."

They turned at the landing. Dolly had to watch her footing. When they reached the top of the stairs, Fiona flicked a switch, and golden light bathed the hallway running off to their left. The green-and-gold carpet runner lapped up their footfalls without a sound.

For a moment, Dolly was somewhere else, blue shadows rippling around her.

"Here," Fiona said. The sensation vanished. They stopped at

a room with an open door. A scattering of glowing blue orbs provided enough light to show the size of the room and the shapes of the furniture. "We can't go in, of course. It's warded."

"It's huge," Dolly said, peering in. It was half again the size of the study. "And mostly . . . empty."

"Yes. Since the war, Daddy's commissions have fallen off. Daddy works best with gold and precious stones, and he can't afford as many of those right now."

"Is he worried about this stock market business?"

"Oh, yes. Daddy *loved* the stock market, and we lost a caboodle on Black Tuesday." She stepped back. "Come see this. It's the absolute *berries*! You'll adore it." She tugged on Dolly's arm and led her farther down the hallway.

They stopped in front of an elaborately carved section of the wall. To the right, at shoulder height, sat a narrow rectangle of brass. Its outer edges were etched with decorative whorls, framing an indentation shaped like a human hand. At the tops of the first three fingers, the indentations were deeper and blue light winked out at them.

"That's odd," Dolly said. "Is it art?"

"Daddy would say it's a *work* of art, no doubt. It's the vault. Only Daddy and Francis can open it. It's an affinity lock. That's blood magic."

Dolly looked from side to side. "Where's the vault? There's no door."

Fiona rested her hand on the carved wood. "This is the door. You can't even see the seam or the hinges, but a rod of unbreakable metal runs through the door and into the wall. It's just like any slide lock you've seen a hundred times, except the rod will only move when the bespelled stones in the handprint recognize the hand. Then they draw the slide bolt to themselves in some way, like magnetism, I suppose, and the door opens."

"Well, but a brutal thief could open this easily," Dolly said. "All they would have to do is cut off your brother's hand or your father's."

Fiona gave a peal of laughter and clapped a hand over her mouth. "Well, aren't *you* a bloodthirsty little thing! That's been thought of. The hand must be living. I don't know how the magic knows, but I guess it's affected by temperature, a pulse and so on. It's very clever."

Fiona continued the tour. Soon, though, she began to yawn without stopping, and Dolly guided her back to the second floor and put her to bed. As she came out of the room, movement caused her to look up. Francis Earnshaw stood in the shadows.

"You startled me," Dolly said softly, closing Fiona's door.

"Is she all right? I heard her chattering in the hallway, and I wondered."

"She is already getting better," Dolly said. "Good night, Mr. Earnshaw."

"You can call me Francis." He made no move to leave. "Did she show you everything? Even the vault?"

"How did you know that?"

"I heard her. I wonder why she showed it to you."

"I think it fascinates her," she said.

"I can see you didn't try to open it, or you wouldn't still have both your pretty hands," he said. "The magic is unforgiving."

"You sound like you know that from experience."

He gave a slow nod. "We've had thieves, once or twice. It's never gone well for them."

"I'll feel quite safe here, then," she said. She nodded and

went into her room. She closed her door firmly, although she had already noted that it had no lock.

Chapter Two

OCTOBER 6, 1929

(SIX WEEKS BEFORE)

VIOLET SOLOMON WAS SLIDING the meatloaf out of the oven when her brother's key turned in the lock. She set the meat on the stove and unwrapped the dishcloth from around her hands. "You all right?" she said.

Philippe closed the door behind him and shot the bolt. He started for the bathroom, flipping his hat onto the couch that doubled as his bed when he slept here. He didn't quite glide, but Violet always saw her brother's movements as fluid, feline, like the puma he shape-shifted into. Still, there was a curve to his shoulders tonight.

"Philippe?"

"Yeah. I watched over the Farrell house for a shift, that's all. Farrell's in the hospital."

"Hospital? Watching the house? What's happened?" Chuck Farrell was a strapping white boy, son of Irish immigrants, who delivered hooch for the same bootlegger Philippe worked for when he wasn't tending bar at the speakeasy. Usually Philippe kept his distance from the white boys. "Why does the family need watching?" She drained the greens and dumped them into a crockery bowl.

"Mr. Chubbs asked me to."

Chubbs paid Philippe on time and called him by his name, but they weren't chummy. Philippe did his job and nothing more. Well, usually, anyway.

"A gang beat him up." He disappeared into the bathroom, and she heard water running as he washed his hands.

She raised her voice. "He drift onto someone else's patch?"

Her brother came back out. He picked up the bowl of greens and set it on the table. "No. They were shouting antlered freak. He said one of them had a lazuli charm, and a couple had silver chains and rifles."

Silver chains to trap him in his animal form . . . A wave of cold swept over Violet as she put the pieces together. "Where was this? Anywhere near *your* patch?"

He shook his head as he sat down at the table. "Bottom of Queen Anne Hill. You know, close to . . ." He didn't finish the sentence.

Close to where they used to live, she and Pedro, her common-law husband, when they ran the botanica on the waterfront, Pedro's botanical magic and her herbalist skills making them a good living until that row of shops burned. "Doucette territory," she said.

Philippe stretched. "Doucettes aren't bootleggers," he said.

"I know. Shim runners."

"Mr. Chubbs doesn't touch shim. This wasn't about the business." Philippe's head turned. "Gabriel's here." A moment later, Gabe's distinctive knock sounded at the door. Philippe flowed out of his chair, his shoulders straightening as he unbolted the door. Just the thought of seeing Gabe filled his body with energy. She remembered the feeling. She envied him.

Gabe stepped across the threshold, his Japanese cedar cane in hand, bringing with him the aroma of fresh bread. Sometimes she worried, along with everything else, that the white man's regular presence in her apartment would raise eyebrows, but Philippe said most of the neighbors assumed she cooked and cleaned for the white man and served him dinner here because it was simpler. And Gabe never spent the night here. They were careful about that at least.

Her brother wasn't reckless, exactly, but when it came to his shape-shifter nature, and Gabe, he wasn't careful *enough*. They never touched each other in public, but plenty of people on the old block knew about him and Gabe. She was sure some of them knew what those marks on her brother's cheeks were too. Violet thought she took risks enough for the both of them, but her brother didn't listen to her about the dangers in his life. He never had, not growing up in Saint Augustine, and not here.

Philippe drew his fingers down Gabe's arm. "Gabriel."

Gabe leaned over and kissed Philippe's temple. "Hello." He drew back. "Hello, Violet."

"How's business, Gabe?" She reached for a plate for him. There was an order to Gabe's plate—she thought of it as the face of a clock. She put a slice of loaf at twelve o'clock.

He came over to the table, touching its surface and locating space before he put down the paper bag he carried. "Business is good. Two protection sigil tattoos this week; I've made the rent." He hung the cane over the back of his chair. Even in this place, where he knew where all the furniture was, Gabe used his cane to navigate. "I brought some bread. How are you?"

"Fine. Philippe had some bad news; one of Chubbs's men got beat up."

Gabe tipped his head, making his short gray braids swing. "Territory dispute?"

"No. Because he was a shape-shifter."

Gabe drew out a chair. "You ever run with him?"

"He's a stag, I'm a cougar," Philippe said.

"So I guess not." Gabe sat down. "There're more and more of those attacks. Was this anywhere near you?"

Philippe snorted. "The same question my sister asked. Nowhere near. Bottom of Queen Anne Hill."

Violet put meatloaf on their plates. While Philippe sliced the bread, she put a scoop of greens at six o'clock on Gabe's plate. "Coming over," she said, and slid it toward him.

"Thank you. It smells wonderful."

For a few minutes, no one talked. Then Gabe said, "Queen Anne Hill. I've heard there's a new shim-running gang challenging the Doucettes."

"They're not so new," Violet said. "Been around since '27, at least. On the east side." Two men had come to the house, years ago, to talk to Pedro about growing shimmer for them. He turned them down flat, but theirs wasn't the only place in that neighborhood with a greenhouse.

"Pushing into Doucette territory."

She nodded then remembered Gabe couldn't see it. "What's that got to do with hating shape-shifters?"

"I don't know." Gabe ate some greens.

Violet sampled the meatloaf. "The White King had another screed about speakeasies," she said. "Waterfront speakeasies, as if we're the only ones in town."

"The *Star-Invocation* prints anything he writes," Gabe said.

"They know which side their bread's buttered on," she said.

"Maybe his daughter should find another place to drink, Violet?"

Violet shook her head. "When she drinks, she talks. It's useful."

"You're carrying your interest in that family a little too far."

"I'm not," she said.

Philippe swallowed then said, "Nobody says a word about the son and what he does."

"Because he's the White King's son," Violet said. She gave her brother a narrow-eyed glance. "You be extra careful out there, Philippe. In fact, why don't you quit delivering hooch at all? I can pay you more if you need it."

His gaze was steady, but she thought there was a buried hint of anger in it. "I like having something of my own, Violet."

"Well, why that? You could find another job."

"I moved hooch for Pedro."

"Not the same thing."

"It pays well. You think I want to sleep on my sister's couch my whole life?"

"I don't like it. They're trolling the streets for shifters now."

He looked down at his plate as he stabbed the meatloaf. "I'm careful."

"Careful! You went and got those marks, right on your cheeks!"

Gabe's own cheeks turned pink, and Philippe laughed. "They barely show, Violet, and besides, no one here knows what they mean."

She pointed at him. "You can't count on that. Haven't you heard them on the radio? Seen them in the streets with their signs and their chants? You know we have to be even more careful than white folks do."

"I know it."

Gabe said, "Violet, he's got my protection sigil. Nobody can make him change against his will."

She transferred her glare to Gabe, even though it was useless. "Your sigil's great. It doesn't protect my brother against a gun, a club, or a silver collar. Or a rope."

Neither man answered her.

"I've already lost one man to this city," she said. "Not doing that again."

~

She never expected to end up on the West Coast, running a speakeasy. Back in Saint Augustine, she knew exactly how her days would go. Her mother and Aunt Lily were both herbalists, and there might even have been a hint of botanical magic in the bloodline, although Violet didn't inherit it. She learned the plants and their properties, while her younger brother did pickup work and helped out. Regularly, Aunt Lily took them out to a shack in the swamp, and Philippe would shift, becoming a swamp puma, or, as they said here, a cougar.

She'd been six when Philippe came along, old enough to think of him as hers in a way. Enough older than him to learn to push down the envy she felt seeing her brother glide through the underbrush, creamy gold and tan, to see how much brighter his smile was, how loose his body was, after a night as the puma. By the time he was six, he'd mastered the change like most shifters did, but there were times when she could see what a struggle it was for him not to let the cat out. "The shape-shifter blood, that had to be your daddy's," Mama said.

"Did Daddy turn into a cat?"

"No, but your granddaddy did."

Daddy'd been a boatbuilder. His parents had helped settle

Lincolnville after they were freed, and Daddy had learned the boatbuilding trade. While his older brother inherited the house, Daddy and Mama made enough money to buy their own in the same neighborhood and bring Aunt Lily over from Georgia to live with them.

One night, Daddy never came home. Philippe wasn't old enough to remember him, but Violet did.

She was young, lively, and her heart had never been snagged, until Philippe took Mama's car in to be worked on. When he went to pick it up, she went with him. She'd grown up hearing about falling in love, but she'd never understood the phrase until she met Pedro. The whole world tilted and whooshed her down like a giant slide into his dark eyes, his wide smile with the crooked tooth on the right side, the warmth of his skin, and the music of his voice. Even though he was of Spanish descent, Mama and Aunt Lily approved of him at first. "That's honest dirt under his nails," Aunt Lily said, after the first time Pedro came for dinner. "Or engine grease at least."

Pedro Avila y Lopez worked as a mechanic, but he was the son of an old Saint Augustine family, gifted botanical magicians. His father had gotten addicted to shim, lost the family home and the orange groves, and died of liver failure.

Mama was less happy when she learned he didn't only work on cars and boats. Pedro kept his botanical skills alive by selling a local bootlegger syrups and tinctures to flavor his rotgut. Soon, Pedro was helping with distribution. Then he was out on his own, making regular deliveries of Canadian whiskey into Georgia.

Mama didn't understand Pedro the way Violet did; he was terrified of debt. He'd been old enough to watch his shim-addict father take out loans against their property and lose everything. Pedro swore that wouldn't happen to him. He'd earned enough money to buy his mama a small house near the cathedral, and as soon as he had enough for a second one, he said, he wanted Violet to marry him. "First a house, querida, so you know I can provide for you. Then the priest and the ring." He bought her a medallion of the Virgin Mary on a gold chain, along with a pair of amethyst earrings.

Mama wasn't pleased. "Pretty words don't count. Standing up in front of a minister, or a priest, that's what counts," she said.

"He wants to buy us a house first," Violet said.

"Then he could stop spending money on flash like those earrings."

"I don't care about words in front of a priest," Violet said. "All I know is I love him and he loves me."

They didn't talk about it after that. In fact she talked less and less to Mama and Aunt Lily. Philippe, who was helping Pedro at his warehouse, was the only one she could talk to.

She didn't understand the business then, and Pedro had always been so careful. She didn't know he had climbed too high, too fast. He started a feud with a bootlegger who came into town from up north, but that man wasn't working alone. He had friends from Chicago.

One night, nearly midnight, Violet woke to the distant sound of sirens, many sirens. A little later, a car door slammed, and someone pounded on their front door. Reaching for the bat by the door, she opened it a crack and peered out.

Philippe supported Pedro, soot covering them, both disheveled and bloodstained. "We have to go," Philippe said. "Grab what you can."

"Wait." Her hands shaking, she still made them stand there while she lifted the black tourmaline wand from its hook by the door and ran it over each of them. There was no magic; this was no illusion. She threw her arms around Pedro. "Are you all right? Are you hurt, either of you?"

"They'll come for us," Philippe said. "Violet, pack. Hurry."

"What happened?"

Pedro choked out words: Tommy Roy and Chucho dead; the warehouse, fueled by barrels of whiskey, vanishing in a vortex of white flame against the night sky.

Aunt Lily came into the room. "Violet?" She reached for the nearest lamp.

"No lights!" Pedro said.

Mama followed Aunt Lily. "What's this ruckus?" Her glance at Pedro turned into a glare hot enough to fry him like a fish. "What have you *done*?"

Violet ran for her room, flung open the closet door, and pulled down her Gladstone bag. Into it, she threw shoes, blouses, skirts, her jewelry, cosmetics, her underwear, and the fold of cash she had tucked away. Her hands shook; she felt cold to her core. What if Pedro had died in that fire? What if Philippe had? These foolish men without enough sense to take care of themselves. She could have lost them both. From the front room, her mother and aunt were nearly shouting.

"Don't you 'Tia Lily' me, you hooligan! What have you brought down on us?"

The bag bumped against her calf as she ran back. Philippe came out of his room, a small leather bag in his hand. He'd done the same thing she had.

Mama stood with her arms folded. "We're going nowhere. Once you're out of here, they'll leave us alone."

Pedro lowered his gaze. "You can't count on that. They aren't like us, these northern gangsters, they have no honor—"

"Honor, *you*? You won't even marry my girl!" Mama pointed at him. "You, Pedro Avila y Lopez, I curse you, your child—"

"Mama, no!" Violet said.

"Violet, tell me you're not—"

Violet marched to Pedro's side. "No, I'm not, but I *will* have his children someday. Don't you dare curse him."

"Can't you see he's a bad one?" Mama said.

"Camille," Aunt Lily said, shaking her head.

Mama sighed, her shoulders slumping, and turned to the tiny desk against the wall. She lifted a small, black leather book from its surface. "Here, take this. You'll need it when he leaves you high and dry."

"I would never—"

Without looking at him, Mama pointed at Pedro. "Not talking to *you*."

"Mama, these are your recipes."

Aunt Lily's voice was soft. "We know them by heart, Violet. Those were always written down for you."

The shaking took her whole body. Fighting not to cry, Violet straightened. "I'll call you when we get somewhere safe," she said. "Mama, I love you."

"I love you, child. Philippe, stay safe and take care of your sister. I love you."

"Love you, Mama."

They followed Pedro out of the house, and got into his car, and drove west until sunrise.

~

They ended up clear across the country, still close to an ocean. Here, magicians had to pass a test and pay a fee in order to make a living, but Pedro obtained the necessary paperwork and practiced botanical magic from the snug little house they rented at the bottom of Queen Anne Hill. Later, they opened the botanica in a neighborhood close to the waterfront. From the shop, they sold lotion, tisanes, and nonmagical items. Those two years were the happiest Violet could remember.

Philippe helped with deliveries and finally found work delivering hooch for a local bootlegger. He got quieter, and his body got tighter, coiled almost. He still moved like a puma but without the looseness, without the smile. Philippe could not change easily in Seattle. Most of the other shape-shifters in town were white, and many were wolf families, and they didn't like other predators. The ones like Farrell, who shifted into deer, didn't like pumas either.

It was the only fly in the ointment at first. As she and Pedro worked and saved, though, they noticed a change in the attitude toward magical practitioners. The neighbors muttered about the Order of Saint Michael the Protector. They made Violet uneasy, but Pedro didn't worry. Like everyone in the neighborhood, they paid a fee to the local councilman, to protect them from burglary, arson, or holdups. "We're safe here, querida," Pedro told her, and gave her a pair of small emerald earrings for her birthday. She knew from his face whenever he came home from confession that the priest was scolding him to marry her, but she wasn't worried. Their savings account grew, and it would happen soon. Violet imagined the future, with the sounds of children's laughter filling the little Queen Anne Hill house.

~

Some neighbors said the blind tattooist was Irish; some said he was from Norway. One thing everyone agreed on: He'd traded away his sight for a set of magical tattoo needles. He worked out of the shop next to theirs, and Philippe was smitten.

Philippe always had a yen for the gorgeous boys who crewed the rich folks' yachts wintering in Saint Augustine, but Violet was surprised when he took up with a blind white man at least ten years older than him. Not that Gabe wasn't charming—he was. It was the only thing she couldn't discuss with Pedro. Pedro loved Philippe like they were brothers, but he pretended he didn't know how Philippe was. He could never find a way to embrace his Catholic faith and accept Philippe. It gave both men in her life pain, and there was nothing she could do about it.

One morning—while Philippe was sweeping the boardwalk out front and Gabe walked back from the diner on the corner, his polished cedar cane swinging—a car pulled up and parked. As Gabe passed in front of the botanica's windows, four men got out and made a semicircle around him.

Violet went to the door, barely able to breathe. Pedro was up at the house. She was alone in the shop. Philippe had set aside the broom and stood tense and straight. As she cracked the door, she heard the unmistakable thud of a person falling.

Her brother lunged forward like a springing puma.

"Philippe, don't!" she said. He jerked to a stop, shaking. He never looked away from where Gabe lay prone, his legs on the boardwalk, his torso in the dirt. Her brother reached for the broom again, gripping it in one hand but not moving.

The white man closest to them looked sideways at Philippe and the broom and let one hand slide under his jacket.

She wasn't sure she could stop her brother if they hurt Gabe worse. And she couldn't stop four white men from killing Philippe if he went after them. It seemed like that was what they were waiting for.

"Don't!" she said again.

Gabe groped for his cane. One of the men shifted it out of reach with his foot.

"I guess you really are blind," said the man standing closest to the car. Violet studied him. He wore a light-gray suit, and the sun turned his hair to a golden helmet. A red stone glinted in his tie. "But you don't mind pushing needles full of colored muck into decent people. How do you sleep at night?"

Gabe levered himself to a sitting position and reached out again for his cane. The blond man shook his head, and this time the man close to it didn't move it. "I'm a licensed tattooist," Gabe said, getting to his feet. He sounded as calm as he always did.

The blond man shot her brother a frowning glance as Philippe leaned forward. "Go back to shining shoes, boy."

Philippe did not answer. He took a step toward Gabriel. The man with his hand under his jacket pivoted so he half faced Philippe.

Gabriel said, "I think there's a misunderstanding. I pay my registration every year. Check with the Commission of Magi. Talk to Councilman Cahill at city hall about my other fees. He'll tell you."

The man close to Philippe said, "We don't care what some stuffed shirt down at city hall thinks. We're here to protect the decent people of the city from the scum who prey on them."

Gabriel's head swiveled as he turned his ear toward the man.

The blond spoke again. "We're here to protect." He nodded, and one of the men took a folded slip of paper from his pocket. He stepped up to Gabriel and tucked it into the front of Gabriel's shirt.

From where she crouched, Violet saw Philippe shudder. He wasn't going to change, but he was struggling with it. If he didn't put the broom down, he might do something just as bad. For all of them.

The blond man said, "Get your darkie protector there to read that to you. Or, if he can't, maybe Cahill can." He turned and strolled back to the car, and the other three followed. They drove away.

Violet threw open the door. "Come inside. Please, Gabe, come inside and sit down."

He did, and Philippe followed him. Gabe sat and tilted the cane against the back of the chair.

"I'll get us tea," Violet said. "Unless . . . something stronger?"

"Tea is fine. Thank you. And Philippe, don't endanger yourself for me."

Philippe put his hand on Gabe's heart, and Gabe covered that hand with his own.

"You should let me give you a protection tattoo," Gabe said.

"They weren't watching me," Philippe said.

"They sure were," Violet said. "Gabe, what's on the paper? May I look?"

Gabriel gave a nod. Philippe drew the paper out, unfolded it, and handed it to her.

"It says *fifteen*. And a date. Three days from now."

"More fees? But you pay already." Philippe stared down at

the paper. "And . . . *fifteen*?"

Violet handed her brother the paper and went to start the tea. Behind her, Gabe said, "I've heard the rumors. Philippe, Violet, the man who spoke. Can you describe him?"

Philippe shut his eyes and concentrated. "Blond hair, wavy gold. No hat."

Violet said, "A red tie tack, a garnet or a ruby. Dressed rich but not flashy like a gangster. He looked like money. Tea, Gabe, right in front of you."

"Thanks." He reached out for the cup. "I didn't know that one's voice. I recognized the other one's, though. He came into the shop a few days ago, acted like a guy who hadn't quite made up his mind to take the plunge." He sipped his tea. "Do me a favor, Violet? Send a telegram for me, to the councilman?"

"Of course." Violet found a pencil, and Philippe jotted down the words Gabriel gave him.

~

Councilman Cahill never replied to the telegram.

Two days later, a man came to the botanica, asked for Pedro, and handed him a sealed envelope. Violet stopped what she was doing as he opened it. He scowled. "I don't understand," he said. "They say I have to register and pay fees for the shop, and they're imposing a fine because I didn't declare it before."

"We don't do magic here," Violet said.

"I'm already licensed as a botanical magician. All we do here is sell and start some seedlings."

"What?" Philippe stood in the door, one hand reaching for the back of his neck. His fresh protection tattoo must be itching. Violet didn't love magic any more than she loved those defiant tattoos on his cheeks, but anything that would keep her brother safer was all right in her book. At least the sigil would protect him from hexes and bad spells.

She filled him in. "It's a mistake," she said.

Pedro rubbed his top lip with his index finger. "I'm not sure it is. Commissioner Earnshaw is calling many people 'magical' even though they have no magic and then squeezing registration fees out of them. They're saying herbalists and botanicas facilitate magic now."

"That's ridiculous. Does a wood-carver who sells a figurine to a magus 'facilitate' magic if the magus charms it later? Are glassblowers facilitating magic? Weavers?"

"Amulet makers register," Philippe said.

Violet stabbed the counter with her finger. "Amulet makers are so specialized, they practically *are* magicians. They're the exception. They've *always* been the exception."

Pedro straightened. "It's just like Prohibition, maybe? Washington passed dry laws years before the rest of the country did."

"They want to make magic illegal?" Violet couldn't believe that. The Commission and its commissioners grew fat off the fees they charged for magic. They wouldn't outlaw it.

"They want to decide who uses it and how," Philippe said. "That's worse."

"I'll go talk to Councilman Cahill."

"He never answered Gabriel," Philippe said.

"What are you saying?"

"He's gotten awfully quiet."

Pedro laced his fingers through Violet's. "I had nearly enough to buy the house for us."

"You know I don't care about that."

He pulled his hand away. "I contributed to Cahill's campaign, and his daughter's wedding was the only one in the city boasting orange trees with ripe fruit, in November, because of my greenhouse *and* my generosity. He'll talk to me." Pedro looked around. "Where's my hat?"

~

Pedro never spoke about how his meeting with the councilman went. Gabe didn't pay the fifteen dollars. For about a week, things seemed normal. She and Pedro stayed late one evening working on a large shipment of a pain-killing lotion Violet made. By the time it was all packaged, the last streetcar had run. They decided to sleep in the back room, surrounded by the smell of fresh seedlings. It wasn't the first time they'd done it.

She woke up, choking, surrounded by smoke. "Pedro!" She rolled over, shaking him. "Pedro, wake up! Get up!" The room was gray; each breath rasped her throat. He snorted, half sat up.

"Fire!" she shouted.

He staggered to his feet. With her arm around his waist, she guided him toward the door. The room felt like an oven. When she could get enough air, she called out, "Help us! Somebody, help us!" hoping Gabe would hear her in the shop next door, where he also lived.

Glass shattered, and a human shape wavered in the clouds of smoke in the main shop. Above her head, a loud creaking ran in a line across the ceiling, and something slammed across her back, knocking her forward and down onto the wooden floor. Pedro grunted. She lay stunned.

Hands grabbed her arms.

"No! Help him!" She turned her head. Pedro lay facedown in the doorway. At first, she thought she only needed to drag him across the threshold, but as she reached out, she screamed, seeing the beam pinning him to the floor and the inferno behind him.

"Violet." Philippe grabbed her and tugged her away from Pedro.

"No! We can save him! We can—" She pushed against her brother, but he dragged her back and back, away from Pedro. She lowered her head and bit his arm, and he cursed. A shudder ran the length of his body, but he didn't change, and he didn't stop.

"Philippe! We can save him! We can—"

More glass shattered, and a hiss like a hurricane filled the room—steam, as neighbors threw buckets of water through the broken window. She heard later they broke down the door and that it took two men besides Philippe to hold her, to keep her from going back in. She remembered nothing else of that night beyond the image of her beloved pinned by the beam, the flames roaring behind him.

They buried his bones and had a Mass said for him.

She and Philippe stayed at the Queen Anne Hill house through the end of the month, the house that would never hear the laughter of her children.

The fire had started in Gabe's shop, along the wall it shared with the botanica. Once it reached the attic, there had been no stopping it. Everyone knew Pedro, Gabe, and two other shopkeepers hadn't paid the Order of Saint Michael. Half the block had burned. Since the war, they all knew about ways to start fires without being present.

For a while she only touched scraps of her life. At Pedro's funeral, a man came up to her as people filed out. He wore a wore a dingy black suit, a bowler, and a Saint Christopher lapel pin. "Miss Violet," he said, holding out his hand. "Lazlo Penske. That Lopez y Avila, he was a competitor. We weren't friends, but I respected him."

Lazlo Penske was a greengrocer in a neighborhood right on the water. He bought some special herbs from Pedro for his elixirs, and Pedro trusted him.

Penske took a slip of paper from his pocket. "I know this isn't the time, but I think you'll want to sell his stock. He had some rare herb seedlings. When the time comes, see me first. Unless you're going to run the business now?"

She shook her head. "I've got no plans to."

"I'll give you a good price."

She took the paper and tucked it into her purse. "I'll call you."

In his will, Pedro left half his savings to his mama and the rest to her. He requested she sell his seed stock to Penske, with whom he had a handshake agreement. There was a hundred-dollar life insurance policy, and she was the beneficiary.

"A hundred dollars," Philippe said. "It seems like a lot."

"What Mama said to him that last night, it stayed with him."

Gabe helped them find an apartment on Jackson Street, not as close to the waterfront as the shop had been. He rented a place across the street and down the block, with a big front room where he could work.

Violet knew they'd moved, but she had lost herself by then. In her mind, she thrashed in a night river, no difference between the starless sky and the water that sucked her down.

Voices howled in the distance, and more than anything, she just wanted to stop fighting, to sink and sink. Sometimes, just as she was about to let herself do that, Philippe's voice reached her. It was the only thing that kept her thrashing.

One night she came back to herself as Philippe yelled at her from the doorway. "What are you doing? Are you even in there?"

"I'm here, little brother," she said.

Tension flowed out of him. "I thought you were hexed or something," he said.

"Not hexed," she said. "Just . . ."

"Not alone," he said. "Never say alone. You aren't."

She looked at him. Sometime, while she'd been in the night river, she knew she'd seen newspapers and pictures in the society page. She'd seen the man who'd shaken down Gabe, the leader of the Order of Saint Michael the Protector, and she knew there would never be justice for Pedro. For a moment, she yearned for Saint Augustine so strongly, it hurt. She wasn't going anywhere. The man she loved was buried here.

She'd never get true justice for Pedro, but even a rich man could have certain problems. She had a way to watch and maybe help those problems along.

They would not drive her out, she decided there and then.

She made her voice brisk. "No. Just grieving. And I know what we're going to do, but I need your help."

"What can I do?"

She drew a set of keys out of her bag. "I need you to go to the central station and the bus station and empty out my lockers," she said. Like Mama, Violet never completely trusted banks.

Philippe took the keys.

He brought back the bundles filled with her jewelry the next day—and watched with curiosity and some concern, she thought—as she went out several nights in a row.

"What are you doing?" he said, standing in front of the door one night.

She tweaked the bright scarf she'd wrapped around her head. "I've got a meeting."

"This time of night? What are you doing?"

She laughed. "Not *that,* Philippe. No, I've got a plan. You and me, we're opening a club."

"A club? You mean a speak?"

She nodded. "We'll have good hooch and velvet booths and a piano player."

"Violet, that takes money. There's people to pay off, and bootleggers . . ."

"I know. I've already rented the shop below us. It used to be a hat shop. Underneath is a basement with an opening into the underground. I've talked to the right people. And tonight I'm getting the final price on a few things, and then I'll sell my jewels, and we'll be good to go."

"A hat shop . . ." Philippe tipped his head. "That could work. Gabriel knows a woman who makes hats. She could even sell you a few so it looks like the real thing." He stepped away from the door and reached for his hat. "I'll come with you."

"You don't need to."

"I think I do. I'll be quiet, don't worry. And . . . Violet? Don't sell the emeralds."

"Why?" She never thought her brother was sentimental.

"They make you look regal," he said.

She snorted. "Regal?"

"Yeah. You're a colored woman opening a business on your

own. Let them know you're someone to be reckoned with."

For a moment, she faltered. "Am I?"

"Oh, yes," Philippe said. "You are."

~

The three of them finished their meal. Violet looked across the table. At least everyone was safe for now. She stood and began to clear the plates. "I'll do that," Philippe said, rising. Between them they soon had the dishes stacked. Violet ran water in the sink.

Gabe came to her side. "I can dry." Once she lay a clean dish on the counter, he would pick it up. They had a system now.

"Good," she said. "Thanks."

He lowered his voice, his face aimed toward the sink. "I don't like the shape-shifter business," he said.

"That makes two of us."

Chapter Three

NOVEMBER 7, 1929

(TEN DAYS BEFORE)

DOLLY OPENED HER EYES to darkness; midnight or a little bit later, most likely. Once again, sound carried to her from across the hall. She threw back the covers, pulled on her dressing gown, and went to Fiona's room. As she reached for the doorknob, she heard the squeak of a window opening.

After a second bad night, Fiona had slept straight through the night before as the effects of shimmer-shim left her body. Dolly thought they were past the worst of it.

She flung open the door. The draperies danced in the breeze. The room was empty, and the window stood half-open. She hurried over to it and looked down. The top of Fiona's head gleamed in the faint light as the girl climbed down the gutter drainpipe.

"Fiona!" Dolly did not want to raise her voice and awaken the entire household, but she projected as firmly as she could. Fiona looked up but continued her climb.

Dolly ran out of the room and down the servants' staircase. *Curse* the girl. She switched on the light in the kitchen. If Mrs. Chambers had moved the key . . . but it was there, hanging on a hook above the icebox. Dolly snatched it and opened the door, barreling into the garden and grabbing Fiona by both arms as the girl turned to run across the soft, green lawn.

Fiona twisted. "Let go! I was just going out for air!"

"Through the window?"

Fiona pulled against Dolly's grip. The yellow light from the kitchen flashed off a bit of metal on her hand. Shadow covered them, and Dolly looked back. Someone blocked the path of light from the kitchen. She recognized the golden hair.

"Fiona? Where were you going?" Francis asked, stepping out into the garden.

"No place," Fiona said. Dolly didn't let go of her arm. The girl had dressed in the wide-legged trousers and a long black sweater. Dolly looked down at Fiona's thin-soled flats. Her own bare toes already tingled from the cold.

"You sister had a night terror," Dolly said. "It's rare but not unheard of with shimmer-shim withdrawal."

"She managed to get dressed, in the midst of this terror?"

"I can speak for myself," Fiona said.

"Well?"

"Well, I . . ." She flashed Dolly a glance. "Yes. Yes, I did."

"There are stories of people cooking meals or even driving vehicles while in this state," Dolly said.

Francis nodded. "Sure. Stories."

"Come on, Fiona. I don't want you to get a chill." Dolly dragged her back to the kitchen door. After a moment, Francis stepped out of the way.

Dolly steered them down the hallway.

"Dolly—"

"Not a word from you," she said to Fiona. "Not one word."

Fiona was silent. Dolly's fingers crushed wool and flesh, and she forced herself to relax her grip. She guided Fiona back into her room, shut the door, and leaned against it. Gusts of cool air wafted through the window.

"That," Dolly said, "was stupid."

Fiona sat down on her bed, pressed against the headboard, and drew up her knees. "I don't want to talk about it," she said.

"We damned well will." Dolly marched across the room and slammed the window. "Just where were you going?"

"To Violet's, I guess. I needed a drink."

"You're wearing scent," Dolly said.

"Yes? I do, sometimes."

Dolly walked over to the bed. "What's this ring? You've never worn it before." She took Fiona's hand. The ring was a narrow strip of gold entwined with small, enameled flowers.

"It's just an old ring. Nothing special."

"Who is he?"

Fiona stared up at her. "What? You—"

Dolly looked at the door and back.

Fiona closed her mouth. After a breath, she said, "His name's Robert. Robert Loughlin. Rob."

"How did he contact you? Or did you contact him? Mrs. Chambers? She's sentimental—is she your messenger? Was he going to pick you up, since you no longer have a car?"

"He wasn't. I was . . ." Fiona pulled her pillow across her knees. "I was going to walk down to the bottom of the hill. There's an all-night diner there. I was going to use their telephone to call him and have him meet me."

"You were going to walk two miles down Broadway Avenue in those shoes." Dolly gestured to Fiona's shoes. "Your feet would have been a mass of blisters. That's a nice note for your romantic tryst."

Fiona began to sob, soft yelps bursting out of her, her face pressed against the pillow.

Dolly walked away from the bed and went into the corridor. Francis Earnshaw leaned against the wall beside her bedroom door.

"I wonder why your father bothered to hire me, when you're such a capable shadow," Dolly said.

Francis's teeth flashed. "I wonder that myself," he said. "Seriously, I can't nursemaid Baby Sister every minute. I have work. The Order of Saint Michael the Protector is important work, Dolly."

"I'm sure it is."

"I can't worry about what Fiona is going to do to embarrass herself."

"Fiona is fine. I'll watch over her."

He said, "You must be a very light sleeper."

"I have to be."

He looked at the door to her room. "Are you going back to bed?"

"I'll spend the night in her room."

He straightened and stroked the breast of his dressing gown, which, in the light, she could see was royal blue. "You have lovely hair, Dolly."

"Good night, Francis."

She went inside and shut the door. Fiona lay curled up with her cheek pressed against the pillow, asleep.

~

Dolly woke with a stiff neck from her slumber in the chair. While she was helping Fiona dress, she noticed a ring of light-blue marks on her arm. "I bruised you," she said.

Fiona shrugged. "I didn't notice." Her eyes were dull. As she pulled a comb through her hair, she said, “I’m sorry. I just . . . I wonder if Daddy will lock me in the attic now.”

“Let’s hope not.” Dolly feared Earnshaw’s reaction would involve sending Fiona into seclusion somewhere.

Earnshaw was not in the breakfast room, but as Dolly finished up her eggs, Inez came in. “Miss, the master would like to see you in his study.”

Fiona jerked and splashed coffee into her saucer. Dolly swallowed and said, “Thank you, Inez.” She stood, her heart pounding, and went into the Earnshaw study, once again facing Ambrose Earnshaw across his wide ebony desk.

“Francis tells me Fiona tried to pull a runner last night,” he said.

“Yes. I thought she was having a night terror. Frankly, Mr. Earnshaw, I had no idea Fiona was so athletic.”

Earnshaw folded his hands. “My daughter does not have magic, or any particular intelligence, but she’s determined,” he said. “Francis thought you acquitted yourself well.”

“I caught her before she embarrassed herself,” Dolly said. “She said something about a boy.”

“Yes. Robert Loughlin. It’s unfortunate, but Fiona isn’t a child anymore, and grown-ups have to do unpleasant things sometimes.”

“He’s not in your social class, I take it,” Dolly said.

Earnshaw shrugged. “He’s with the police, and his father is a judge, but he isn’t magical. The purity of the magical bloodline is one of our greatest responsibilities, Dolly. You’re not magical yourself, so perhaps it’s hard to understand the importance of that duty.”

“Oh, it isn’t hard at all,” Dolly said. “How did Fiona manage to meet a policeman? He didn’t arrest her, I hope.”

"They met here," Earnshaw said, after a pause. "His father, as I said, is a judge. As the commissioner, I needed some advice on a magical matter, and Judge Loughlin was very helpful. I was so focused on our discussion, I did not see what was happening farther down the table."

"So Fiona might have thought he was, at least, an acceptable prospect."

"My daughter didn't think, I'm afraid. She let her passions fly away with her."

"Perhaps if someone spoke to this young man . . ."

Earnshaw shook his head. "He is as unreasonable as she is. He has taken a dislike to Francis now and has . . . accused him of things. He won't listen." He straightened, and Dolly could tell he was about to announce a decision.

"I think having Fiona here in town is a poor solution," Earnshaw said. "We have a cottage on Orcas Island, in the Sound. We'll move her up there until the engagement party at least, or perhaps until the wedding."

Dolly's stomach dropped. She looked at her lap. "All things considered, that's probably for the best," she said. "We can't count on mere respect for parental authority to affect her behavior, after all, not when there is a young man in the picture."

"Yes," Earnshaw said. "Well. What do you mean, 'respect for parental authority'?"

"As Francis pointed out to me last night, you and he are both important, busy men, with responsibilities. Everyone knows that. People can't expect you to control a rebellious daughter. Removing her from the social setting that causes the temptation is a logical solution. As the wedding grows closer, she can come into town for fittings and such things. No one would question it much. Absence from this young man will give her plenty of time to reflect on how poor a match it is."

"Absence . . ." Earnshaw leaned back in his chair. "Yes. Exactly." The leather sighed as he shifted his weight. "On second thought, I think we are seeing improvement, don't you?"

"Oh, yes."

"Well, let's not be in a rush to make a dramatic change that may not be necessary. A change in routine, it could even set her back, isn't that so?"

"It might," Dolly said. "The conservative approach is always good."

"Well, then." Earnshaw reached for his newspaper.

She picked at a cuticle with her thumbnail. "Mr. Earnshaw, this may not be the best time, and this isn't easy for me, but there's something I must discuss. I think perhaps I should not stay in the house. During the day I—"

"What?"

"I must find another place to sleep."

Earnshaw's bushy brows knit. "What? We have an *agreement*! I'm not angry with you, Dolly. I think you did as well as could be expected last night. What's this about?"

"I understand the attitudes of the wealthy can be different and more permissive, but I don't have the luxury of living that way. My reputation is all I have, and I cannot feel comfortable at night in a house where one of the men practices invisibility."

"What?" Earnshaw gaped then leaned back in his chair again. He started to laugh. It sounded like an animal roaring.

When he paused for a gulp of air, Dolly said, "It isn't a joke, sir. It leaves me in an uncertain position."

"It's not invisibility, Dolly. Francis has the ability to veil himself if there is a nearby shadow, that's all. It's a minor skill. I'm sorry if he's disturbed you."

"I . . ." She stared at the edge of his desk and did not finish her sentence.

"Dolly, you are safe here. I hear everything that goes on in this house. Francis is just playing. And you're a capable young woman. I'm sure you can handle him if it comes down to it."

She sighed and didn't speak.

"I'll speak to him about it. Please don't give it another thought, and do *not* give another thought to leaving."

"Very well," she said.

He took up the newspaper, dismissing her, and she rose and left the room silently. In the foyer, once she knew she was alone, she drew a long, deliberate breath.

~

NOVEMBER 10, 1929

(SEVEN DAYS BEFORE)

Dolly went down to the kitchen at about seven thirty. She was in the habit of getting herself toast and coffee and reading the *Seattle Star-Invocation* until Fiona joined her in the dining room for breakfast.

Mrs. Chambers was usually whisking eggs and laying out bacon, but she wasn't in sight this morning. As Dolly pulled the loaf of bread out of the box, she heard soft voices from the back door and walked toward them.

Mrs. Chambers stood with her back to Dolly, talking to a lithe, young colored man not much taller than she was. She looked over her shoulder. "Oh! Miss Dolly!" She turned back to the man and said loudly, "And you tell him, young man, I want *new* turnips. That last batch was old enough to vote!"

"Yes'm." He nodded, nearly a bow, and stepped back.

Mrs. Chambers shut the door awkwardly. "I'll just be a minute, Miss Dolly. I have to put these in the pantry." Her left arm was folded tight against her apron, holding something in place.

"Not to worry. I just wanted to be sure everything was all right." Dolly went back to the counter and sliced the bread.

"Just the grocer's boy," Mrs. Chambers said. She seemed out of breath as she poured out a cup of coffee.

Dolly kept her attention on the bread. "You know, Mrs. Chambers, if a hardworking woman has a wee dram in her room once in a while, a nightcap, it's no business of mine."

"Ah? Well." Mrs. Chambers blushed. "Shall I bring your coffee out to the dining room?"

"Yes, please. Has the paper come?"

"I put it out for you."

Dolly was skimming the society page when Francis came into the room. "Here's the early riser," he said. He reached over and picked up the front section of the newspaper.

"Good morning." She did not look up.

Fiona entered, yawning, and sat down next to Dolly. "Bacon smells good this morning. Anything interesting in the paper?"

"Skirts," Dolly said. "A bit longer for spring, the experts think."

Mrs. Chambers set a plate with a fried egg and three rashers of bacon in front of Fiona, who murmured thanks. Dolly poured out some coffee and handed it to her charge.

"And a wolf attack in Pike Street Market," Francis said.

"A wolf? In the market?"

"A *wolf*, Fiona. She transformed in the middle of the market and attacked several people. Bit a man's arm so badly, she broke a bone. They got a silver net on her, finally."

Fiona's eyes got wide, and she set down her coffee cup. "Shape-shifter?"

Without looking up, Dolly said, "It's a strange story. More interesting for what's not written down than what is, I think."

"What do you mean?" Francis walked around the table behind Fiona and took a piece of bacon off her plate. He crunched it, chewing vigorously.

"I knew of wolf families in San Diego," Dolly said. "The O'Malleys, for instance, were pillars of society. They even paid for a wing of the veterans' hospital after the war. They did transform into actual wolves, I believe. Anyway, the families teach their youngsters to control the transformation from an early age, and they rarely travel alone. The family is everything to them."

"Well, if Dad were here, no doubt he'd say . . ." Francis threw out his chest, puffed up his cheeks, and lowered his voice half an octave. "Nice clothes and expensive homes are no substitute for character."

Dolly looked up at him then returned to the paper.

"Why would she *do* that?" Fiona's voice trembled a bit. "Didn't she care that there were people around? I mean, aren't they just animals when they change?"

"Certainly the animal nature is ascendant, but if they were 'just animals,' how would they change back? They are usually careful."

"Then why just change on whim, in such a crowded place?"

"But they *don't*, Fiona." Dolly folded the paper. "It's very rare. That's why I think this story is incomplete. What if something provoked her into changing?"

"Perhaps the storekeeper didn't have what she wanted." Francis smiled as he took a second piece of bacon off his sister's plate. "You take quite an interest in wolves."

Dolly put one hand in her lap and clenched her fist. It wasn't worth her while to get angry at those kinds of remarks. "I like facts."

Fiona shivered. "It's frightening."

"Well, it's far from us," Dolly said. She picked up her coffee cup.

"We'll keep you safe, Fiona," Francis said. He smiled at Dolly. "We'll keep you both safe."

"Are you eating, Mr. Francis?" Mrs. Chambers said as she came in with a rack of warm toast.

"No time, Mrs. Chambers. You two girls have a good day. And take care." He sauntered out of the room.

~

After breakfast, Dolly suggested they walk in the neighborhood and perhaps Volunteer Park. The morning's drizzle had stopped, and the clouds evaporated. Fiona had been free of the effects of shim for a few days, and she was a sharp and funny companion with a soft spot for dogs. They walked in the park for over an hour and sauntered back to the house, Fiona nodding to the maids and housekeepers they passed.

Earnshaw met them in the foyer. "Fiona, I've chosen a date for your engagement party: December seventh."

Panic flitted across Fiona's face. "That's less than a month away."

"Yes. Do you want it at the house or at a hotel? The Roosevelt has a lovely ballroom."

"I don't know, Daddy. There is so much to plan, I don't think I . . ."

"Nonsense. You have Miss White to help you."

"A hotel puts most of the bother on the hotel staff, rather than you and your family," Dolly said. "It's easier for the society page reporters to be there. People like arriving in public, showing off their fancy duds to the photographers."

Fiona snorted. "Very true. Well, let's consider hotels." She gave her father a narrow-eyed look. "I don't think the Roosevelt is necessarily the thing, Daddy. It's a bit old hat. Stuffy."

"Let me know what you decide."

"Perhaps Inez can call some of the better hotels. After lunch we'll tour them and see what's on offer," Dolly said. "Mr. Earnshaw, do you want Francis to come along, or would you like to join us?"

"I don't think either will be necessary, Dolly. You'll have the chauffer if you encounter any . . . problems."

He turned, straight-backed, and went into his study.

Fiona's eyes widened. She stood on tiptoe, cupped her hand around Dolly's ear, and whispered, "You must teach me how to manage him!"

~

The white-and-gold phaeton's long nose and sweeping running boards gave an impression of aggressive power its smooth ride belied. Fiona and Dolly lounged against the soft leather seats. The glass vase mounted on the back of the front seat held a small, white hothouse rosebud. They were on their way to the Olympic, the most modern hotel in the city.

"Should your fiancé have a say in the planning?" Dolly said.

Fiona shrugged. "He'll be fine with whatever I choose."

"You . . ." Dolly glanced at Nick, the chauffer. "Do you care for him?"

"I do. We're friends. We just . . . don't love each other. Think of us as the children of two royal families, cementing a political alliance."

"That's medieval," Dolly said.

"That's Seattle," Fiona said, "at least for magical families. Daddy believes strongly that we must marry and produce children so the affinities are not lost."

"And the Arbelios, they're magical?"

"Oh, yes. Tony's magical, and I have the bloodline. We'll make a respectable couple." She sighed and looked out the window.

Dolly said quietly, "But there's Rob."

"There used to be."

"Well, that's just heartbreaking."

Fiona laughed and shook her head, but it was an unconvincing laugh.

"So you sought out gin and shim."

Fiona plucked the rosebud out of the vase and began to twirl it. "Isn't this pathetic? We aren't here to talk about my broken heart, Dolly. We're planning a party."

They drove for half a block. A sedan passed them. Fiona turned her head, following it, then faced forward. She twirled the rose bud again.

Another block along, Dolly leaned forward. A group of people, in two lines, marched up Fifth Avenue toward the hotel. She counted eight men and two women bringing up the rear. The women held signs, but she couldn't read them. "What is that?"

"Oh, those are happening all over," the chauffer said.

"What are they saying?" Fiona rolled down her window. Dolly could read some of the signs now. SAVE OUR CHILDREN! NO MORE WOLVES!

The chanting, or singing, reached them.

No more wolves!
No more wolves!
No more wolves,
In our hometown!

"You haven't heard that song, Miss Fiona? It's all over the place."

The marchers fell away behind them.

Dolly said, "Something tells me you know every bit of that song."

Nick glanced up at the rearview and gave a slight shrug. "I may know a verse or two." He began to sing in a smooth baritone:

We're taking out the shape-shifters,
Every one we see,
With nets of magicked silver,
And a spear of laa-zoo-lee.

We're cleaning out the dirty wolves
And every mutt that speaks,
We're bagging all the killer cats
And all the antlered freaks.

No more wolves!

No more wolves!

No more wolves,

In our hometown!

"What started all this dislike of shape-shifters all of a sudden?" Dolly said.

"Well, no one's ever liked 'em."

"I don't see why. They're just another form of magicker."

Nick glanced up at her again. "That's not true. They've told us for years that they're just people who change, but anyone who's met a shifter can see they're more like jumped-up animals. You can't trust an animal. And they fought against us in Germany."

"There were wolves in the American army and the British army," Dolly said. "They risked wounds and even sacrificed themselves to save their fellow soldiers. They just didn't get medals at the end of it like others did."

"How could that be, Dolly?" Fiona said. "They wouldn't fight against their own kind."

"They didn't. They were Americans," Dolly said.

Nick shook his head. "You've been sold a bill of goods, Dolly. They never fought on our side. Clannish, they are."

"No more so than many others. Look at the magical families."

"But, Dolly, they're dangerous. Look at the woman in the market," Fiona said.

"I think that poor girl was probably crazy before she shifted, and she'd have run just as mad in human form."

"Yes, but she broke a man's arm."

It was Dolly's turn to shrug.

"Well, I'm just glad there aren't any in our neighborhood," Fiona said, putting the rose back in the vase.

"Yes, thank goodness."

Fiona gave Dolly a sidelong glance and frowned but didn't say anything more.

Chapter Four

FIONA TOOK TO THE hotel manager at once, and soon the three of them, having inspected the ballroom, were studying menus and tasting samples brought out from the kitchen, preceded by the scents of bacon, chicken, brandy, and beef. Shim suppressed the appetite, but Fiona's was fully back now, and she nibbled with obvious enjoyment.

After a second taste of the tender squab Véronique, Fiona looked away, smiling in an embarrassed manner. "Excuse me just a moment," she said. She hurried from the room.

When she didn't return, Dolly excused herself too. She admired the lobby as she walked through it, with its glittering chandeliers and the shining filigree work along the mezzanine railing. Outside, parked diagonally across Fifth Avenue, sat a black sedan with the outline of a gold shield on its door. Dolly looked from side to side and spotted the mouth of an alley close to Seneca Street.

Fiona was there, twined around a man. Dolly stopped, feeling the instinctual pinch in her gut at the sight of his blue uniform. Fiona's fingers were wound through his black hair, and her face was tipped up against his as if she were drinking nectar pouring from a flower. From the hips down, their bodies joined like one.

Dolly took her time approaching them. "Don't you have menus to be studying?"

They untwined with a jerk. Fiona blinked as if she were drunk. The man turned half away from them, adjusting the waistband of his uniform trousers. He was tall and wide-shouldered, with a narrow, supple waist.

Fiona said, "Dolly, this is—"

"I know who this is. Go back inside."

He turned now to face Dolly and put out his hand. "Miss White, I'm Robert Loughlin."

"You're the one who's gotten Fiona in a lot of trouble," Dolly said. She did not take his hand.

Apart, even now, their bodies leaned toward each other like strands of underwater kelp. "Just one more minute, Dolly. Please," Fiona said.

"If your father gets wind of this, you'll be on an island in the middle of Puget Sound until your wedding," Dolly said. "Go."

"Go, darling," Robert whispered.

Fiona bit her lower lip. She pressed her hand against Robert's cheek and stepped away from him. Before she was out of reach, he grasped her hand tenderly and kissed the tips of her fingers.

"Oh, for crying out loud," Dolly said. "You two aren't star-crossed lovers in a movie."

Fiona ran past her, her cheeks bright pink.

"She told me you'd help us," Loughlin said.

"I have no idea why she told you that," Dolly said. "Come along, Officer Loughlin. I'll walk you to your car."

He didn't look embarrassed or defiant. He met her gaze straight on with eyes the color of a chocolate bar. Of *course,* Fiona had fallen for this one.

"I love her, Miss White," he said.

"That's delightful. She dove headfirst into a gin bottle because of you, Mr. Loughlin. There is no reason to think you are any better for her than Tony Arbelio is."

He faltered. Perhaps his shoulders slumped a little. "Maybe I'm not. Tony's a good guy, even if he's a bit of a daisy."

"Why do you say that?"

Loughlin raised his eyebrows. "There are certain clubs that a certain kind of man . . ." He hesitated. "It's not my place to talk about it. Point is, Fiona deserves better than being sold like livestock."

She stepped over a crack in the pavement. "Magical families are different. Those like us don't measure up."

He stayed at her side. "I measured up fine the first four months. Good enough for dinners, card parties, excursions, while the White King persuaded my dad to support him with the city council."

Dolly turned. "Your father made a ruling in favor of Mr. Earnshaw?"

"Of course not. He'd never do that. But Earnshaw wanted stronger penalties for unlicensed magickers. Before, practicing without a license always got you fined. Now a second offense gets you dropped in the hoosegow for sixty days. City council was divided on it, and they all respect my father. When Earnshaw got the vote he wanted, suddenly I wasn't good enough for Fiona anymore."

They stopped at Fifth. A trolley rolled by in front of them. From its window, a man lighting a cigarette stared at them, especially Dolly. She did not stare back. She hurried across the street with Loughlin at her side.

He stopped by the car door. She could see his billed policeman's cap resting on the driver's seat. Loughlin said, "You don't know them, Miss White. You've been taken in by the house and their manners. Francis is trouble in a sharp suit, and the White King's worse."

"And you'd like to get back at him," she said.

He shook his head. "No. He'd always told Fiona she should expect to marry into a magical family. But he threw us together. He let her, he let *us*, hope. He shouldn't have. *That's* why the gin, Miss White. Because he let her hope."

She looked at him. What a lovely pair of fools he and Fiona made.

"You think Fiona would be happy on a policeman's salary?"

"She'd be happy with me," he said.

So certain. She shook her head. "I don't know, Robert. I think maybe you're the kind of man who'd like a tragic love in his past. So you can moon over the society pages and sip your whiskey, thinking about what could have been and never having to find out if you two could have weathered a marriage."

"You're coldhearted," he said, "and you're wrong."

"Coldhearted, yes. As for wrong . . . Ask yourself this. If she were just Fiona, who had to get a job in a shop and learn how to cook and to clean, would you love her as much? No—" She held up her hand as he opened his mouth to speak. "No passionate speeches of undying love, Robert. Talk is easy. Just think about it. Would you stand by her side?"

She turned and walked away. He might have called something after her, but a jalopy rattled past, and she couldn't hear his words.

~

Fiona hummed to herself in the car back to the house. Glancing at Nick, Dolly said, "You seem pleased with the Olympic."

"Oh, very!"

"And the menus. Those offerings were tasty."

"Oh, yes, *so* tasty. I *loved* the offerings."

"It's settled, then."

Fiona stopped humming. She reached for the rosebud but drew her hand back. "Yes. It's settled."

The parade of chanters had vanished. Fiona leaned forward. "Nick, I meant to ask. Who is Laa-zoo-lee?"

"What, Miss Fiona?"

"In the song."

"I don't know."

"I think it's a reference to lapis lazuli," Dolly said. "It's a blue stone."

"Really, like a sapphire?"

Dolly shook her head. "It doesn't sparkle. It's deep blue with a matte finish. You've probably seen it in jewelry, especially Egyptian style."

"Egyptian style?" Fiona's brow crinkled. "Maybe I have."

"With a gold setting, with the right spell, it reacts to shapeshifters."

"Like silver?"

"Not exactly. It helps identify them."

Fiona nodded. "Oh, like black tourmaline."

That wasn't quite right, but Dolly didn't correct her.

Over dinner, Fiona described the Olympic to her family. Earnshaw agreed it sounded acceptable and said he would go inspect it later in the week. Francis smiled at his sister. "You are almost like your old self again, Fiona."

"I feel as if I've come out of a fog," she said. "As much as I dislike that awful stuff Dolly made me drink. Speaking of coming out of a fog, where is your blessed medallion? I haven't seen you wear it in a while."

"It's at the jeweler. The clasp broke."

"Oh." Fiona pushed away the last bit of her lemon custard. "How did that happen?"

"Stop quizzing your brother," Earnshaw said.

"I was just *asking*."

"I'm not six, Fiona. Stop fussing."

"I'm sorry," Fiona said. "I think Dolly and I will have our coffee in the drawing room. We have a party to plan. May I be excused, Daddy?"

"An excellent idea." Earnshaw stood up. "I'm going up to my workroom."

Fiona waited until her father had left. "Dolly, shall we?"

Francis stood aside as his sister brushed past him. When Dolly neared the door, he reached out and put his arm across it, blocking her. "I owe you a great deal for the return of Baby Sister."

"If Fiona is happy, and your father is happy, those are all the thanks I need," she said. She stood calmly, looking at him without blinking.

"You're a lovely woman, Dolly. Maybe the fog is clearing for me too."

"It's good to be clearheaded," she said. "Excuse me."

He let his arm drop, and she went past him toward the drawing room. Gradually, her heartbeat slowed.

~

NOVEMBER 13, 1929

(FOUR DAYS BEFORE)

Without as much need to watchdog Fiona, Dolly had some trouble filling her time. Once or twice, she ran errands for Mrs. Chambers. Fiona enjoyed morning walks, and Dolly walked with her, as well as walking again before sunset. It kept her limber and sharp. She had, with Earnshaw's permission, taken one evening off to hear a lecture on natural science at the library and spent a few hours one day at an art museum.

Now she was the one to have trouble sleeping. She would say good night to Fiona and wander into the drawing room, reading or jotting notes for the engagement party, but sleep eluded her.

This night was no different, and still awake and restless although it was past midnight, Dolly went downstairs to choose a book from Earnshaw's library. Earnshaw was out, spending the night at his club, and Francis had left after dinner, whistling as he pulled on his jacket.

She tried the study door, thinking Earnshaw might have locked it. The knob turned easily, and she stepped in, touching the toggle on the wall to bring up the ceiling light. The room was cool.

The French doors were ajar, and light from the house next door, filtered through the yew tree hedge, threw long streaks onto the floor. She walked over and pulled the doors closed, twisting the latch. As she turned to the bookshelves, a shape filled her vision, and she started, gasping. "Francis! Where did you come from?"

He grinned at her, standing at the end of the couch. "And where did *you* come from, wandering through my father's study like you own it?"

She kept her gaze steady. "He said I could use his library."

He strolled toward her. "You can use anything in this house you want."

She mastered the impulse to step back. "And what are *you* doing here?"

He grinned. "I live here, Dolly." He moved so close, she could smell cologne, cigar smoke, and whiskey. "You manage things well, don't you?"

"What do you mean?"

"Well, you've weaned Fiona off gin and shim and kept her away from that awful downtown speak. She's even focused, finally, on the marriage. All because of you."

"It's barely been two weeks," she said. She skirted him, approaching the shelves. "And it's my job."

He caught her arm and held her still. "You know I *saved* your job, don't you? I could have told Dad you weren't diligent in watching Baby Sister."

She tugged but could not pull free. She had underestimated his strength.

He said, "You were so eager to stay here, close to me. You played Dad like a fiddle to keep Fiona here. Why so chilly now?"

"You think that had something to do with you?"

"Well, why else? The house doesn't offer anything for you."

"It was your father's decision," she said.

Francis laughed. "He'd already had Inez bring Fiona's trunk down from the attic. Ten minutes with you, and plans are changed. It wasn't his decision. It was yours."

"I can't convince you," she said. "As to what there is for me here, I need a job."

"A beautiful woman never needs to worry about a job," he said. "I'll take care of you."

"Spoken like a rich man trying to get a woman into bed," she said.

He let go of her and strode to the study door. "Francis," she said, hurrying after him, but he pulled the door shut and locked it. She stopped as he turned with a smile. "Open the door," she said.

"I don't like games, Dolly. Not this kind—coy girls' games. You came right in here, when everyone else in the house was asleep."

"I didn't know you were here."

He grabbed both her arms and dragged her against him. "Then we'll call it fate."

"Let go of me."

"After a kiss." He bent his head down. She stamped her foot on his instep as hard as she could.

He straightened and drew his arm back as if it were a tennis racket. She turned her head to avoid the worst of the blow, but the momentum knocked her down, and she fell, her ears ringing, against the end of the couch.

"Do you think you can say no to me?" He stood over her, staring down, his face half in shadow, still smiling. "Is it *Dad* you're holding out for?"

She gripped the edge of the sofa and pulled herself into a half-sitting position. "I bet I'm not the first woman you've hit," she said.

"What?"

"Maybe not even the first woman this month."

He reached down and caught her by the neck. Something pulled in her spine and numbness spread down her right arm.

He hauled her up, and she clung to his hands, trying to pry them free. He was too strong.

"You watch your mouth," he said. He pushed her back onto the sofa, falling with her. His weight was on top of her. Black and red spots danced in her vision, and the blood began to rush in her ears. She fumbled with her left hand for the pocket of her skirt. The pressure in her chest doubled, and the black dots swept in.

Her shaking fingers found the smooth capsule in her pocket. She pulled it free. All she could feel was his sweating weight.

She reached up toward his face, the slick capsule between her thumb and forefinger, and crushed it.

Too late, he snapped his head sideways. The gleaming golden powder shot up his nostrils with his inhalation. Dolly drew up her right leg and shoved it into his midsection with all her remaining strength. He slid sideways off the sofa.

She fell onto the floor. Her body screamed for air, but she made herself crawl two arms' lengths away, free of the oblivion powder, before she opened her mouth, gasping so hard, it sounded like sobbing. The terrible pressure eased. She rested her forehead on the soft carpet. Her neck ached, and her arms trembled.

She sat up and rubbed her arms. Her right thumb prickled like it had gone to sleep. Francis lay insensible a few feet from her. She crawled over to his side and tilted his head to the right. On his neck two faint lines showed, nearly healed. They might have come from fingernails.

Dolly pulled two preservation vials from the pocket of her skirt and uncapped them. Tensing her fingers, she raked her nails down Francis's neck twice, right over the marks, until blood filled the shallow furrows. She decanted blood and flecks of skin into each vial, capped them immediately, and sat back, still gasping.

In some ways, this was easier than she'd planned, if more dangerous.

But what had he been doing here, coming in through the garden? Clearly, he'd used his veiling illusion. Where had he been? Where had he come from?

She gripped the points of his collar and ripped down hard, spraying buttons. She unbuttoned his fly for good measure. Then she walked behind the sofa.

She found a square gap in the wainscoting, just above the floor. A secret drawer. Francis had lowered the illusion that hid it, and a small metal box hung half out of the drawer. She opened it cautiously. Inside she found a fold of bills and counted them quickly; nearly five hundred dollars. She put them in her pocket. There was a lock of black hair, a plain silver locket, and a brown notebook. She picked it up and riffled through the pages. Dates in one column, nicknames in one, and figures in the farthest. *Oh, Francis,* she thought. *You're a bigger fool than I realized.*

She tucked the book into her pocket, slipped the box back into place, and closed the secret door.

~

Fiona sat up, startled, as Dolly came into her room and turned on the bedside lamp.

"Dolly? Is everything—"

Dolly put a finger to her lips and sat on the edge of the bed. Fiona sat up.

"What happened to your neck? Are you all right?"

"Your brother tried to throttle me."

Fiona stared. Tears filled her eyes. "I did try to warn you. Oh, Dolly, I'm so . . ."

"Hush. You had nothing to do with it."

She looked at the door. "Has he gone?"

"He'll be oblivious for a few hours. I think his memory will be very hazy. And I think we'll leave it like that."

"Are you sure? I could talk to Daddy."

"Doesn't he already know? He hears everything, doesn't he?"

Fiona blinked. "I don't know. He says he does. When he's *in* the house at least, but . . ."

"So." Dolly held a hand to her throat. "Would you find me some valerian? Please?"

"Yes, right away." Fiona got out of bed and ran down the hall.

Dolly slipped the notebook into the drawer in Fiona's nightstand. When Fiona came back, Dolly was leaning back in her chair, rubbing her bruised throat. "I guess this makes us even," she said, smiling, as she pointed to the fading bruise on Fiona's arm.

Fiona said, "Will you be all right?"

"I will," Dolly said, tipping down the valerian tincture and following it with a swallow of water from the glass on the nightstand.

"Does this change things?"

"It changes nothing," Dolly said.

PART TWO

GRIFTER

Chapter Five

OCTOBER 4, 1929
(SIX WEEKS BEFORE)

THE BON MARCHÉ SAT proudly on its new lot at Third Avenue and Pine Street, reaching up four glorious stories. The cream of Seattle society did not shop at the Bon; instead, the successful and upwardly mobile came there, buying the clothes they hoped would boost them into that elusive top drawer.

Dolly strode past it to a narrow alley running alongside the department store. Tall buildings cut out the sun, and here, it was ten degrees cooler. The paper-wrapped parcel draped over her arm crackled slightly with each step.

Her steamship had come in the night before. She had found a room in a boarding house, ladies only, and paid four weeks in advance. A quick job authenticating some magical artifacts for an old client in Astoria had given her a pretty good stake, but this job would be pricey, and she didn't know how long it might take before she found a way inside the Earnshaw home. Some economies were in order.

The small shop she sought had a simple sign: a wooden silhouette of a dress. A bell tinkled as she pushed the door open. The smell reached out and engulfed her, a mélange of old perfume, soap, hot irons, and fabric. She waited for her eyes to adjust.

Every society wife knew about this shop or one like it. Sometimes even wealthy families fell on hard times, and sometimes last year's clothes were not given to the servants but taken and sold to someone whose watchword was discretion. Sometimes the family fortune was intact but a society wife or daughter had a bootlegger to pay off, an important medicinal potion to procure, or a special friend to keep in jeweled cuff links and fine shoes. The buyers who came here were very different; usually young, sharp-eyed girls with a bit of cash in their worn purses and a willingness to gamble for a higher place in society.

Jackets hung along one wall. She recognized several years' worth of styles, but an enterprising girl with a good eye and a good hand with a needle could make something fine from any one of those. She walked toward the back.

The shopkeeper, a gray-haired woman with a steady, gray-eyed gaze, watched her approach. "I'm not buying today," she said. Her tone was friendly enough but firm.

"I might be."

"Ah."

"I think you should have a look, though. You'll kick yourself later if you don't."

"I'm old and stiff," the shopkeeper said. "I don't often kick myself."

"I'd hate to think I made you start." Dolly set the parcel on the counter and waited.

"Well, let's see it then."

She unwrapped it slowly. The travel suit had cost as much as a fur coat. She loved its moss-green color and the silk linen fabric, the careful stitching on the lapels. The jacket was long, with a belt of the same color, and the narrow pleats of the skirt made her seem even taller. She had deliberately chosen a style a bit longer than the trend, and she had never regretted it. The plain black buttons, instead of gaudy gold, down the front added to a sense of understated elegance.

The suit fit her like another skin, almost like a magical one. And none of that mattered. Dolly White would not own such a garment. She could not afford it, and she was not a sleek, killer heron or regal hawk. Dolly White was a sparrow.

"Lovely detail," the shopkeeper said. "Lovely fabric. The topstitching is perfect. Paris?"

Dolly nodded.

The shopkeeper named a design house, and Dolly nodded again.

"Well, it's certainly fine." The shopkeeper stepped back and crossed her arms. "A bit too fine, I think. Most of my girls would fear it was stolen. It's a lovely piece I'd never sell."

"Look at the seams," Dolly said.

"I don't need to. I know they're twice stitched." The woman was shaking her head, but one hand stroked the skirt, shaking out the pleats.

Dolly leaned forward and smiled. She lowered her voice. "Here." She lifted the lapel on the jacket. "Smell."

"Smell?"

"Smell it."

The woman turned her head, frowning, but after a few seconds, she leaned forward cautiously and sniffed the fabric. "Lemon verbena?"

Dolly let her voice drop even lower, speaking softly, the way a woman might when she spoke with her lover, deep in the night. "Close your eyes and smell it again. Draw in a nice, deep breath."

"Why?"

"Trust me."

The shopkeeper shrugged and leaned down. She closed her eyes and inhaled slowly through her nose.

Dolly kept her voice soft. "Do you smell it? That's the smell of adventure."

The shopkeeper stood and opened her eyes.

"The girls who cross your threshold are ambitious. They're adventurous. They have their eyes set on positions far above their stations, and they like to dress for those positions. Most of them fail and end up working their days in a factory or a shop. They marry and have a flock of kids. Some come to scandal and ruin. But some, *some*, succeed, and they climb to a lofty perch of influence and money. You know this. You know *them*. Hang this suit in your window, and there will be a girl it calls to. And she'll answer it, and she'll pay whatever price you ask."

The shopkeeper folded her arms on the counter. "Well, it's an original bit of patter. I'll give you that."

Dolly waited calmly.

"It must be magicked, then."

Dolly waved a hand. "Check it. It's not magicked."

The woman pulled a long chain from under her blouse. A length of black tourmaline hung in a tasteful silver setting. The shopkeeper held it out over the jacket, an inch or so above the fabric, and ran it back and forth in methodical sweeps. She did the same for the skirt. The suit was not magicked. It didn't have to be.

The shopkeeper dropped her charm back under her blouse. "It's a risk, and the risk's all on me. I'll give you two dollars for it."

Two percent of what she had paid. It was about what she

had expected. She nodded then folded the suit aside. "What about the blouse? Silk, with Belgian lace points on the collar," she said, shaking out the glowing fabric.

"Well, aren't you sly? I'll give you a quarter for it."

The deal done, Dolly shopped carefully, choosing a gray suit, some well-made white blouses, a plain frock, and a pair of gloves. The shopkeeper nodded as she brought them up. "You have a good eye, but I'd have thought you'd go for something a bit showier, especially since you had money for a bespoke Paris suit. You don't seem to have slid so *very* far."

"Some of us plunge and some of us slide, but it's still a decline."

"You've a got a silver tongue. Are you Irish? Or did the fairies bless you while you slept?"

The shop seemed colder for an instant, filled with shadows. Dolly stopped a shudder with effort. "I'm not Irish," she said. "Make sure the suit gets into the right hands."

"That I'll do."

Back in her room, Dolly shook out the gray skirt. She stretched the back of the skirt tight between her hands and rubbed it back and forth against the edge of a chair seat until the fabric pilled, looking softer than the rest. With her nail scissors, she carefully picked out the thumb seam on one of the gloves then stitched it back up, making sure a few of the stitches showed.

It was close to sunset. Time to visit an old friend.

~

Marguerite Dillon's house was a neat little two-story cottage, built forty years earlier, in a quiet part of town. The deep porch welcomed guests, and Marguerite herself opened the door to Dolly.

She stepped into the white foyer with its glowing cherry parquet floor. Two long rooms flanked the foyer and the simple white staircase. To her left, she knew, was Marguerite's studio. Dolly imagined a comfortable divan by the window, a cluster of chairs, and a pair of delicate tables. Beyond the four dragon-and-peony screens would be Marguerite's work area: A set of triple mirrors, a sewing machine, dress forms tucked into a corner, and bolts of fabric, lace, and ribbon. A tall apothecary cabinet, imported from China, held beads, rhinestones, buttons, and brilliants in its army of small drawers. Dolly had only seen the house once before, but she knew how Marguerite liked to work.

Marguerite led her into the drawing room on the right. Rather than sleekly modern, this room was old-fashioned but comfortable, with beaded lampshades and overstuffed furniture.

Marguerite also defied fashion convention, despite being a highly successful dressmaker for the wealthiest women in the city. Dolly's business associates in Baden-Baden after the war would have described Marguerite as zaftig, and she dressed to accentuate her narrow waist, plump hips, and full bosom. She wore a dark-red enamel butterfly pin on her pale-blue blouse. She'd made red her signature color and always wore a bit of it somewhere.

"Enid will be bringing in tea," she said, sweeping her hand at one of the chairs. Dolly sat down. Marguerite kept one servant, her housekeeper, Enid, who brought tasty snacks and tea—and sometimes a forbidden bit of sparkling wine—to the ladies as they were having their fittings.

"Business must be good."

Marguerite sank onto the sofa in a cloud of billowing sky-blue silk. "Business is excellent."

Enid came in with a japan tray. She nodded to Dolly and set it down, laying out a pair of plates, white napkins, and spoons. Marguerite might snort at the contemporary fashions, but the teapot was a heart-shaped, green-and-white Art Deco piece. The tray also held tiny sandwiches on soft white bread.

Dolly, who had saved a few pennies on her voyage here by skipping meals, could have used a chop and some boiled new potatoes, but she didn't let that show on her face.

"You've had some bad luck." Marguerite filled Dolly's cup. "Sugar?"

"No, thank you. Yes, very bad."

"Even you can have a failure now and then, Dolly. It is Dolly, isn't it?"

"Yes." She sipped her tea. "It's still Dolly, Daisy."

Marguerite grinned. "Well, a marguerite *is* a daisy."

Dolly inclined her head.

They'd met and gotten to know each other in Omaha, where they'd worked as cigarette girls and lookouts for a club owner. Daisy was an expert seamstress who had come west and invented herself as a master dressmaker, making mouth-watering frocks and gowns for the denizens of Millionaire's Row.

Dolly set her bone china cup on the silver-rimmed saucer. She could have brought her green suit to Marguerite to hold for her instead of parting with it. Perhaps she'd been too quick to get rid of a useful tool, even it had helped defray her expenses.

She put the thought aside and picked up a tea sandwich.

"I'm glad things are going well."

"Quite well, and I owe it all to you. I haven't forgotten."

"Not *all* to me," Dolly said. She had staked Marguerite's business with the take from a successful job. It never hurt to have a society dressmaker beholden to you.

"Well, I owe you enough, certainly. What can I do for you? A wardrobe?"

"Unfortunately, no. I'm curious about a family. It occurred to me that you might know them. The Earnshaws."

Marguerite nodded in mid-sip. "The White King. Yes, I used to dress Blanche, and I still make dresses for the daughter, Fiona, poor lost soul."

"Lost?"

"Oh, she's trying to drink her way to the bottom of a bottle. It started about six months ago."

"Because of her mother's death?"

"No, Blanche has been dead for five years. I think it's man trouble in Fiona's case."

"Well, tell me about the mother. All of them, actually."

"Blanche was a Bartelle, of the shipbuilder Bartelles. Second only to the Morans, and the Bartelles diversified better, so they held on to their fortune after the war. They're mer-magicians. You probably saw their shipyard on your way in."

Dolly took another bite of her sandwich. Mer-magic was a popular name for aquamancy, and she could see how it would help a shipbuilding family.

"A fine woman. She was good for me. She told people she liked my frocks better than those of her Paris dressmaker."

"That's an endorsement," Dolly said.

"It made a difference, believe me. Blanche brought most of the money to the marriage. Ambrose, he had to scrape a bit at first—lots of skill but not much scratch, at least not until he landed those government contracts and got his patents."

"War contracts."

"Yes. He's brilliant with gem magic, and from what Blanche said, he's a bit of an elementalist too. Certainly his listening gems seem to work like elemental magic. His remote fire, that was *very* popular on the front." Marguerite freshened her tea. She tilted the pot toward Dolly, who shook her head. "And he's got a gift for the stock market, where he put most of Blanche's money. It seems to have paid off."

"Did he have anything to do with her death?"

"Oh, I don't think so. The lung condition she died of is common in mer-magicians. Her grandfather died from it."

"Her money came to him, then."

"There's a trust for Fiona, I think. She's the only one in the household with no magic, although it never seemed to bother her."

"What's she like?"

"Before she vanished into a hooch haze, she was a beam of sunlight. She's smart enough, although you wouldn't think so at first. A bit rebellious when it comes to fashion. I made her three pairs of beach pajamas. I don't think her father quite approved. She's quick to have a laugh, quick to poke fun at pomposity—a trait her father does not appreciate. She always treated me well. Lately . . . well, I've seen her twice, and she barely spoke."

"Sullen?"

"Polite enough, but I could smell the gin from across the room. She's . . . numb." Marguerite set down her teacup. "The brother Francis is dangerous."

"A heartbreaker, is he? I shouldn't wonder, with all Daddy's money."

The dressmaker leaned forward. "I'm serious, Dolly. He's hard on women."

Dolly laughed.

"It's no joke. He's got a trick, invisibility or something, and a mean temper. If you're going to take a run at them, keep out of his reach. He's got a type, girl, and you're it. He likes them tall with dark hair."

Dolly shook her head. "Any other gossip about this naughty boy?"

"He got himself a little gang of ruffians who shake down the waterfront magicians, and his father protects him."

"That all-powerful father," Dolly said.

"He is. He controls the Commission of Magi, and they are squeezing out the unlicensed magickers. Even people who aren't magicians, just on the fringes. I think most of the time, he's pleased with his son's gang. They can do what he can't."

"He can't be pleased with the daughter's antics. Where does she get her hooch, do you know?"

"She likes speaks. There's one called Violet's Hat Shop. It's near the waterfront, pretty high-class, I hear. Fiona's mentioned a 'new hat,' and it's clear she doesn't mean haberdashery. I'm worried about her, honestly. I think she's spiking her drink with shimmer-shim."

"That could kill her."

"Like everyone who's riding down that road, she's been warned, but she doesn't care." Marguerite fiddled with her plate. "Dolly, if you're thinking of stealing from them, I'd think again. The house is warded, and there's talk of a safe that's more than unbreakable. They've had a couple of burglaries, and it hasn't ended well for the thieves."

Dolly gave a careless shrug. It was one she had practiced. "I might just be thinking of settling down. It's like the Wild West up here, isn't it? There might be room for a girl like me."

"Just be careful."

"They seem like an isolated family, all alone in their castle. What about mistresses? Did the White King ever cheat on his queen?"

"At least twice, from hints Blanche dropped, but he was discreet and didn't embarrass her."

"How gallant. Anyone now?"

"The whispers are there's a girlfriend. He's been known to"—Marguerite cleared her throat theatrically—"'spend the night at his club' a couple times a week."

"But he hasn't remarried."

"Oh, she's not of his social class."

"The poor man. All alone on his pinnacle."

"He's generous, they say. He's donated a lot to help wounded veterans, and he contributes to a school for licensed magickers, but he has only a few friends. He and Mortimer Lester, they go way back, back to when he first came here. Mortimer's not magic, but he came from money, and he took Ambrose up right away, introduced him to the Bartelles. Lester's in real estate. And one or two members of the city council dine with Earnshaw and play golf with him on occasion."

Dolly rolled her eyes and let her head drop to one side as if in a stupor. "For crying out loud, what a bore this man is!"

"Unless you're trying to make a living as a magicker, or an herbalist, or curandera," Marguerite said. "Then you might find him a little too interesting. Do you have a place to stay? My guest room's available."

Dolly stood. "No, thanks. I have lodgings."

Marguerite stood too. "Clothes?"

"You're a temptress, but no. Thank you."

They started for the door. Dolly cleared her throat. "You might see me again, and if you do, it would be better if you didn't recognize me."

"Of course." Marguerite opened the front door. She turned and smiled. "And Dolly? I hope you know, if the White King sends his officers, or others, to question me about you, I'll tell them everything. I can't afford to be on that man's bad side."

Dolly leaned in, kissing the air half an inch from Marguerite's cheek. "Dear Daisy. I'd expect nothing else."

~

By ten o'clock that night, she'd had her fill of coffee. At the first diner, after she left Marguerite, she'd ordered a chicken sandwich. At all others she'd had coffee, with one stop to use the diner's toilet. Now the streets were dark, slicked by a brief rain shower earlier. Along the way she'd learned about several speakeasies, none the one she needed.

She was looking only for all-night diners now. It was not the best time for a woman alone to be out, especially not in this slightly disreputable neighborhood. At the corner, light from one more place painted the street.

She checked the street and crossed. The window of Jack's Place was steamed up. Inside, it smelled of cooking grease and old coffee, but the red-and-white tiled floor was clean enough to squeak under the soles of her shoes. At the curve of the counter, a single customer sat in profile to her, hunched over his plate. The counterman looked up as she entered.

"Coffee, please." She took a seat.

He slid a thick mug across to her. She stretched and sighed *aaaah* melodically.

"Tired, miss?"

"I arrived today, on the steamer. It was a cramped voyage. I'm exhausted."

The man at the end of the counter turned his head. She kept her gaze on the counterman, but even without looking, she knew the other man was sweeping his gaze up and down her body. So tiresome, yet unavoidable, she supposed.

"Where'd you come from?" the counterman said.

"San Diego."

He shook his head as if to say he'd never been there.

"It's lovely, but a girl needs to stretch her wings." She sipped her coffee. "I can't help thinking about the days when a girl could find a bit of refreshment after a long journey. Against the law, of course, but weren't we a bit, well, more *civilized* back then?"

"We've been dry a long time up here, but we'd get them in here sometimes—the Bright Young Things, we called them. This place would be jumping after midnight. Bacon and eggs, hash browns, gallons of coffee. Not so much now. People coming off swing and night shifts mostly."

"It seems sad."

"You want a little snort?" The man at the end of the counter stood up. He ambled over and sat down on the stool next to her. He wasn't bad looking. He was just intruding.

"Oh, no. No, thank you." She fluttered her fingers. "We're just talking."

"This town was wide open when I was a kid," the interloper said. "I remember Chief Roy Olmstead, the biggest bootlegger of them all, and his wife, Aunt Vivian, on the radio. Between the teetotalers and that Council of Magic, whatever it is, it's sewn up tighter than a nun's—sewn up tight. In the old days, you could get anything you wanted on any street corner."

"Provided, of course, it was the right corner."

Dolly grinned at the counterman's comeback. "Well, we're homebodies, basically, but I do miss the gaiety of the old days."

"You like gaiety?" The interloper leaned in, exhaling wintergreen.

The counterman leaned against the counter, his hands flat on the surface.

The interloper was hitting his stride. "I know just the place. It's a supper club. You can get a steak Diane with maître d' butter and all the champagne a pretty girl like you can pour down her throat."

She swiveled to face him. "Do you think I'm pretty? I'm not the beauty in my family. My sister Priscilla is."

He leaned back on the stool and looked around the diner. "I don't see her."

"Well, of course not. She's back in our room. She and the landlady are listening to the wireless."

The counterman's fingers moved, tapping. *Tap,* a pause, *tap, tap, tap, tap-tap tap-tap.*

"Bring your sister along," the interloper said. "We'll make it a party."

"Are you sure?" She picked up her spoon and began to stir her black coffee. The spoon struck the sides of the mug. "She really is beautiful, and she's got a voice that charms nightingales." *Tink-tink tink-tink. Tink. Tink-tink-tink.* "The chair won't be a big problem, will it?" She looked up at him through her eyelashes.

"Chair?"

"Oh, yes. She's in a chair. Polio."

"Oh." He looked away. "That doesn't sound . . . I don't think she'd be comfortable."

"What a shame, because I couldn't go without her."

"Your loss, then, doll." He stood and tossed a quarter on the counter. She faced back to the front. The door clicked shut.

She looked down at the brown surface of her coffee. When she glanced up, the counterman raised his eyebrows.

"Sister, huh?"

"Well, she's not my sister, but I do know her." Priscilla *was* beautiful, with a voice like aged bourbon, and she was in a chair. She was Dolly's go-to forger. Someday, the law of odds said there should be a man who would call her bluff and be willing to meet the sister in the chair, but the ploy hadn't failed her yet.

"You seem to know your way around."

"I didn't *just* fall off the farm truck."

"Well." The counterman unscrewed the lid of a saltshaker. "I can't help you with the first thing, you know. It's against the law." He picked up a box of salt and poured a thin stream into the shaker. "But I imagine a lady like yourself enjoys getting a new hat from time to time."

"A hat."

"Yes. Perhaps one with a nice flirty brim would suit you. There's a hatmaker down near the waterfront. Violet's. Very modest shop, you could walk right past it and not know it's there, but she makes fine hats." He set down the box and screwed on the lid.

"A hat might be just the thing."

"She's a colored gal. Would that bother you?"

"Few things do," Dolly said, "and that's not one of them." She slid a nickel across the table for the coffee.

"Tell her Abner sent you," he said.

~

Violet's Hat Shop sat on South Jackson Street. The place was dark, but the streetlight highlighted three ladies' hats in the window. Dolly gave the knock Abner had shown her.

A moment or two later, the lock clicked, and the door swung open. A girl peered out. Her straw-colored hair was in neat braids, and her dress, while worn, was clean. She wasn't much older than thirteen. "Shop's closed, miss." Black tourmaline hung on a chain around her neck.

"I'm in need of a hat, though. Abner sent me."

"Abner?" The girl looked her up and down. Dolly had not been a lookout at her age, but she knew plenty of girls who had been. "Well, come in, then. Miss Violet's still in the back, and she might be able to give you something off the shelf." She held up the stone. When Dolly nodded, the girl swept it around her then stepped back and held open the door.

Dolly entered the shop. Yellow light bloomed as the lookout turned on a lamp on the counter. The redbrick walls held only a few shelves, mostly empty, and the place smelled of wool and something floral, perhaps the scent of Miss Violet's namesake. The girl vanished into a darkened back room.

Dolly waited. Because she was listening for it, she heard the low thump of a door somewhere below her. A minute later a woman came through the doorway into the shop. For a moment, she was a figure of gold and shadow. Then she moved into the lamplight. Emerald stones dangled from her ears, and her hair was covered with a twisted scarf in gleaming green and gold. The ends of the scarf formed a flower shape over her left ear. Her sleek dress repeated the colors in a pattern like the eye of a peacock's tail feather. She was an inch or two shorter than Dolly, and her skin was brown. "You say Abner sent you?"

"Yes, he said a girl who'd like a nice hat with a flirty brim should come to Violet's Hat Shop."

The woman folded her arms. "Well, I do have very nice hats, but we're not open. And I don't know you."

"I wouldn't expect you to. I've only arrived from San Francisco. I got in late yesterday."

"And went straight to Abner's?"

"Oh, no. His was the seventh diner I tried."

"Really?" The woman tilted her head. "You must have particular taste in . . . hats."

"I do. I look for special qualities, and I'm willing to pay for them."

"What's your name?"

"Dolly White."

"Never heard of you."

"You may have heard of these." Dolly gave her two other names, one from a job in Seattle a few years earlier and one from Portland, where she had acquired some magical artifacts for a collector.

The woman rubbed her arm. "One of those rings a bell. Tell you what, come back tomorrow. I'll be getting a new shipment in, and we'll see if we have what you want."

Dolly liked that the woman was cautious, careful to protect her operation. She smiled. "Tomorrow, then. Same time?"

"Everything the same. Maureen here will know it's you."

Dolly nodded and left. The girl closed the door and shot the bolt behind her.

~

She spent the next day at the city library, reading up on the city's golden families. She called up the old editions of the papers and read the society pages with care. Dolly knew how to see between the words for what was coded and what was deliberately missing. What she discovered necessitated a telegram to Marguerite, who replied with a telephone number and the name of a man who sold men's shoes.

She sent a telegram to her client in Wichita, confirming merely that she had arrived in Seattle. He was a wealthy collector who desperately wanted a void mask to round out his collection and was willing to pay very well for it. If she was successful here, she'd earn enough to dodge the powerful, angry client she'd left behind in San Francisco for a year at least, long enough for her trail to go completely cold, even for him.

After ten, she went back to the hat shop and gave the knock. Maureen let her in, and the proprietor was waiting for her, still in the shadows. Tonight she wore a hat and dress in shades of bronze and gold. "People know you," she said. "They say you're all right."

"Good."

"They say lots of other things too. Are they true?"

"Which ones?"

"They say you visited the Fair Folk when you were a child."

"Oh, yes." Dolly made herself smile pleasantly. "That one's true."

"How did that happen?"

"The same way it does with most children, I think." She

pushed away the sudden memory of her sisters' faces, painted red by the light of boiler, as they shoved her into the rotting cupboard in the basement, as they slammed and blocked the door. "I got lost. I wandered in the Twilight Lands, and soon they found me."

"How long were you there?"

Dolly shrugged. "That depends on who you talk to. I thought it was about a month. According to my mother, it was three years, but she was a lush, so her word can't really be taken as gospel."

The woman's eyes narrowed. "Do you think the *you* that came back is—"

"Oh, I'm human," Dolly said. "Changed, yes. But human."

"All right." She turned.

Dolly followed her back through the dark stockroom. She was not surprised to see a burly man standing in the corner.

"A friend of Abner's, Tom," the woman said. "Dolly. Make a note." She pulled down a lever in the wall, and the basement door opened with a sigh.

Music swirled out.

The room glowed with golden light. Small, circular tables dotted the floor, and red velvet booths hugged the old red bricks of the wall. There was a dark-skinned piano player riffing something of the new music, jazz, and the lithe bartender behind the polished bar was two shades darker than the proprietor. Everyone else was white. White and well-dressed, Dolly couldn't help noticing. All the women were in couples or groups, and there wasn't a blond to be seen. Fiona Earnshaw was not drinking here tonight.

"Is your gin real?" Dolly said.

The woman grinned. "It's not brewed up in a bathtub, if

that's what you mean."

"Do you cut it?"

"I flavor it. I have training as an herbalist."

"Shimmer-shim?"

The grin vanished. "If shim's what you want, I'll have Tom escort you right back out. I won't have that shit in my place."

Dolly nodded. "Good. I'd like a gin, neat. And what's *your* name?"

"I'm Violet. Welcome to Violet's Hat Shop."

~

The next evening, Dolly stepped out with the shoe seller Marguerite had recommended, going to a supper club called the Pageant. Dolly slipped Trevor the envelope of money discreetly when they were settled in the cab he'd ordered. He was slender, blond, with eyes as blue as bachelor's buttons and an earnest handsomeness, exactly what she needed—a male escort who would raise no eyebrows and would not challenge her virtue while she was working. He knew enough to not ask questions either.

The hostess beamed at them, giving Trevor a wink, and guided them to a table near the dance floor. She had a hennaed spit curl in the center of her forehead and two on her left cheek. Dolly exclaimed over the beautiful ring she wore on her right hand, and the hostess blushed and held it out for Dolly to admire.

She and Trevor enjoyed their meal and took a couple of turns around the dance floor. While the band took a break, Trevor approached the clarinet player, and Dolly visited the powder room. When she came out, she chatted with the hostess for a few minutes, until Trevor came up to meet her. He was grinning. They were both quite satisfied with their evenings.

The pieces of Dolly's plan were dropping into place.

~

Two days later, she watched over the top of her newspaper as Mortimer Lester strode across the dining room, pausing once or twice to shake hands with men at other tables. He was stocky, although he looked firm, not flabby. She had read that he played tennis. His skin was pale, his sandy hair thinning at the top. She imagined his hands were manicured.

The maître d' led him to a booth, probably his usual table. A waiter appeared immediately. Lester gave his order without looking at a menu. Dolly made a mental wager that it would include a large serving of beef. He began leafing through a folder he'd drawn out of his portfolio.

Once he was settled, she got up and made her way to his booth. She knew she was drawing some stares, and not just because of how she looked. The black-and-white day dress was flattering, and her dark-red sash at the waist and the matching hat made her stand out, but any woman alone in a public dining room still drew looks and often comments. Without speaking, she slipped into the booth across the table from Mortimer Lester. She let her hands rest in her lap.

"I'm sorry, I don't believe I . . ." He studied her face. ". . . know you," he finished in a warmer tone.

"You don't yet, but we're going to become great friends."

"I'll be the judge of that," he said, smiling.

The waiter approached, carrying a tray with a short glass holding about an inch of amber liquid and a soda siphon.

He did not hesitate as he reached the table. "Your drink, Mr. Lester, and anything for the lady?"

"Just a glass of water, please," Dolly said.

When Lester nodded, the waiter sketched a shallow bow, deposited the drink, and left.

Lester ignored her, pressing the handle on the soda siphon. A jet of frothy water whooshed into the glass. "I prefer to eat lunch in peace, young woman, so if you have something to say, talk fast."

She smiled slightly and folded her hands on the tabletop. The light overhead made the ring on her right hand sparkle.

Lester, who was sipping his drink, swallowed hard and put the glass down on the tablecloth. "Where did you get that?"

"This?" She held it out, admiring the modern design. Bands of platinum formed a parabola, perhaps a flower or a bow, paved with red and white stones. "From a young woman named Ruby. She's a hostess at a supper club. Of course, she doesn't know I have it."

The waiter reappeared. He set a plate covered with a slab of rare beef in front of Lester, alongside two smaller bowls. One held potatoes and the other cauliflower. He put a cut-glass tumbler filled with water in front of Dolly. She smiled up at him.

Pink flushed up Lester's neck and into his cheeks, making him resemble his lunch. "How *much*?"

"For this?" She drew the ring off her finger and set it on the white linen between them, keeping her fingers on it. "For *this*, nothing." She moved her hand.

He snatched it up so fast, it was almost like a magic trick, stuffing the ring into the breast pocket of his jacket. Glaring at her, he sliced off a triangle of beef, speared it, and chomped on it. She watched him closely. It would be awkward if he started to choke.

"It isn't the only thing I took, naturally."

When he spoke, his voice was congested. "This is a shake-down."

"Of course it is." She took a sip of water.

He snorted and relaxed a little. She'd thought he might.

"The letters? Do you think the police care if a businessman has a bit of skirt on the side?"

"I doubt anyone would care about your love notes, Mr. Lester, although they certainly are *vivid*. The newspapers would never *print* the letters because of the decency laws, but it's amazing how word gets out. If you made Elouise a laughingstock, she might take the boys and move back to Connecticut. I doubt that's what you want."

He ate more beef. He still felt confident, as she expected.

"Again, though, the letters aren't the only thing I took."

The beefy color dropped out of his cheeks. He put down his fork.

"Take a sip, Mr. Lester. You look like you need it."

He grabbed the whiskey glass and gulped down the contents. "You're trying to bluff me. I'll have you arrested, you little tramp. You don't have anything else."

"When a man pays the rent on a place, he thinks of it as his own, doesn't he? Maybe even more than his Queen Anne Hill mansion, the one he shares with his family. He might hide something at that rented place, behind the nightstand where he keeps his socks and underwear. Where even Ruby doesn't know."

His face got paler.

"I do have it, Mr. Lester. I do have the ledger where you

keep track of your *other* business, the one you're trying to expand. And that, I think, the police will be interested in."

For a moment, he couldn't draw a breath. He fumbled for the drink glass, and she handed her water over to him. He took two long swallows. "What do you *want*?"

"You had a great-aunt down in California, didn't you? Tarzana. She died recently. There were no other relatives."

"There's nothing left of the estate, I swear—"

"But there was a caretaker, the final six, mmm, no, eight months of her life, wasn't there? A companion. Your great-aunt Minerva spoke highly of her, and the one or two times you spoke to her on the phone, you were impressed with her competence."

He shook his head, his moist forehead wrinkling. "No, there was no . . ."

Dolly leaned forward. She spoke gently. "Of *course* there was. *You* remember her."

He stared. "Maybe I do."

"She's come to Seattle to look for work. And she'd be just the person to help your old friend Ambrose Earnshaw with his troublesome daughter. Couldn't the Earnshaw girl benefit from a companion? A steadying influence?"

He pushed himself back against the booth, and the whites showed all around his irises. "Ambrose? *No.* No, I could never lie to him. He'd see right through me. You don't know—"

"All you have to do is share a letter and tell him what your aunt told you. It's not much of a lie, Mr. Lester. You won't even have to say you ever met her."

Dolly opened her purse and took out a letter. She unfolded it and flattened it on the table so Lester could see it. She wasn't completely sure, at this point, that he was able to concentrate enough to read it.

Dear Mr. Lester;

I hope you remember me from our telephone conversations when I was helping your Aunt Minerva before she passed on to her heavenly reward. I found there was nothing for me in California, and I have come to Seattle. If I could prevail upon you, do you know someone who needs a companion or nurse? I have good potion skills, and I am honest and reliable. I can also sew and mend if it is needed.

I hate to impose, but I remember how kind you always were to me when we spoke.

Very Truly Yours,
Dolly White

"Shall . . . shall I . . ." He reached for the letter, and she slid it back.

"No. I'll send it to you by mail. This afternoon, after you meet me at the city library. You're going to tell me everything you know about your great-aunt."

"And you'll give me back the ledger."

She laughed. "Oh, no. I won't be doing that. What if you felt compelled to unburden your conscience to your good friend? No, I'll be keeping the ledger and the love notes."

"I . . . Fiona is like a daughter to me. If you harm her . . ."

"Yes, I know how much your set values its daughters. Fiona will be unharmed." She knew he needed a rationalization for betraying his friend. Let this be it, then, that Fiona wouldn't be harmed by Dolly's presence.

She slid off the banquette and stood. "This evening, at five, at the library," she said. On her way out, she waved to the waiter, who smiled back.

Chapter Six

OCTOBER 11, 1929
(FIVE WEEKS BEFORE)

DOLLY SIPPED HER GIN AND THYME and scanned the speakeasy. There was no sign of the Earnshaw daughter, but she noticed the man at the back corner table. She'd seen him here her first night too. He had a sheaf of narrow silver braids just touching his shoulders, and a cane hung over the arm of his chair. One or two people a night approached his table. Plainly he was some kind of magicker.

Curious, she slipped off the stool and walked to his table. He tilted his head as if picking out her steps.

"Hello. My name's Dolly White. May I share your table for a few minutes?"

He nodded. "I'm Gabe. Gabriel Malek." His eyes were clouded as if the whites had grown across the irises. She'd never seen that before. This close, she could smell magic on him. It wasn't coming from him but from something he carried, and not an amulet or a blessed medallion. This was a tool.

She pulled out the chair and sat down. "I'm trying to figure out what kind of magic you do."

He smiled. He was not exactly handsome, but there was something compelling about him. The gray hair created an impression of greater age, but she thought he wasn't yet forty. She couldn't always tell a person's age, just as she wasn't sure about her own.

"I'm a tattooist."

"Oh. Well, I admit, that's not an answer I was expecting."

His smile widened. "And you're not alone there."

"You use magic," she said.

"I was a tattooist before I traded away my sight," he said. "I was skilled. Now I'm more than skilled."

"The needles you traded your sight for, they're magic," she said.

"How did you know that? Did Philippe tell you?"

"Philippe?"

"Violet's brother."

"Oh, the bartender? No. I have a nose for magic. And you're carrying the needles with you."

"Yes. I keep them close now. I give powerful protection sigils, and the needles . . . let me know things."

"Can you make a living at it?"

"The sigils are what I'm known for, if you can afford me, so yes, I'm comfortable."

Tattooed protection sigils were the priciest, and best, magical protection around. An adversary couldn't yank one off your body the way they could an amulet or a charm. Of all the tales of tattoo magic, one set of needles came up over and over, in stories and in history. She said, "You have *those* needles?

"You know of them?"

"Heard of them, at least. Anyone who's been in the acquisition business has. They take . . ."

"They take what you value," he said. "I knew what I was *prepared* to sacrifice, but that wasn't what they took. I'm a walking warning about magical deals."

"How do they work with you?"

He shook his head. "For protection sigils . . ." He thought for a moment. "When I bargained with the needles, I had to walk a labyrinth. The needles take me back to it, the client beside me. At least, that's what it seems like. People say I go into a trance."

Dolly nodded. He'd bargained *with* the needles, as if they were conscious beings. That fit with the stories too. "And the other tattoos? 'Mother' inside a heart, an eagle's head? Do you see those in your mind?"

"As I said, I'm expensive. I don't usually get the bunch of drunken boys daring each other to tattoo a lady friend's name on their chests. But occasionally . . ." He shrugged. "I sometimes tell people I see the image in my mind or that the needles 'show' me things, because that's how people with sight think, and they can understand that. But I feel the design in my fingers, like a line of heat. I can't explain it any better than that. And people aren't always happy, because the needles give them the tattoo they need, not necessarily the one they wanted."

Capricious magic, she thought.

He slid his fingers across the table until they touched his beer glass, drew it toward him, and took a sip. "I don't need magic right now to know you want something, Miss White, and not just a comfortable table to drink at or a magic folktale."

"I'm hoping to meet someone here, but I'm also looking for a greengrocer." Everything she'd discovered so far pointed to an affinity-lock safe in the Earnshaw house. Those took very special handling.

"Hmm. Violet could help you with that. She's left the business, but she still keeps up on it."

"Violet was a greengrocer?"

He took a long sip and a swallow. "An herbalist. She and her man ran the botanica next to my tattoo parlor. He was killed in the same fire that took my shop."

"What happened?"

"We didn't pay the right people."

"Do you know who did it?"

"Know it, can't prove it. The ones who did it were nowhere near the neighborhood when the fire started."

He carried his magical needles with him now because were too valuable to risk again. She said, "I read about something recently, used in the war. Remote fire."

The tattooist nodded. "That's the best known. Anyway, Violet can point you in the right direction." He swirled his beer then set the glass down. "Would you like a tattoo, Miss White? My tattoos tell people things about themselves. For instance, it can answer that question."

"What question?"

"The one that wakes you in deep in the night some nights. Not very often, because you've built an iron box around it. But once in a while, it shakes the box."

It took her a second or two to make herself sound amused. "*That's* what you do! You're a fortune-teller!"

"No. The needles don't tell people their futures. It gives them what they seek."

"That's why you gave Philippe the leopard spots on his cheeks?"

"You recognize those?"

"Not such a smart choice."

"Well. Two years ago it didn't seem as stupid. And even if it had . . . well, I can't refuse that man anything."

"Ah. It's like that." She pushed back her chair.

"Does that bother you?"

"Few things bother me, and that's not one of them. I'll go ask Violet about greengrocers."

"Are you sure you don't want a heart, Miss White? Even a small one?"

"I beg your pardon." She couldn't quite control her voice this time. "I have a heart."

"I meant a tattoo. It could be discreet. On your ankle, the small of your back, invisible unless you choose to make it seen."

"No. Thank you." She stood up. "I don't mean to sound highfalutin, but this body is my instrument. My canvas, so to speak, and the only one who is going to mark it is me."

He smiled and inclined his head.

She knew she shouldn't lash out, but he had cut too close. Sweetly, she said, "Do you miss it? Your sight?"

The smile faded, but he looked thoughtful, not angry. "I do wish I could see the fireworks on the Fourth of July here," he said. "Philippe says they're great, and I hate the noise. It just brings back the war for me. So I'd like to see them. But I'm doing well. We all miss the things we leave behind a little bit, don't we? Don't you?"

"Me? I'm not missing anything." She sure couldn't count *this* conversation as a victory. She shouldn't have poked him in the first place. "I appreciate your help," she said, turning away.

The bartender stared in in her direction as she walked back to the bar, but he wasn't watching her, he was watching Gabe. Whatever the tattooist felt for him, it was reciprocated. Dancing on the edge of a volcano, those two.

"The tattooist said you can recommend a greengrocer," she

said, sliding in next to Violet.

"What do you need?"

"Things that are high-end, rare, and expensive. I can pay." If Violet wasn't in the business herself, there was no need to share details.

Violet sipped her drink. The liquid was clear, like Dolly's gin, and a sprig of fresh thyme adorned it. Violet always made a show of drinking as she moved through the crowd, visiting with her customers, but all her drinks were clear, and she never smelled of hooch. The glass could have held gin, or it could have held water. "I might know someone. He's, well, he's not easy. I'd need a finder's fee."

Dolly nodded without speaking.

"Twenty-five."

Dolly did some quick calculations. The economizing—selling her suit, limiting the cost of meals—all helped. Still, the items she needed were costly. Trevor had been a necessary expense but not a small one. And now a finder's fee . . . "If I use him," she said.

"Fair enough. I'll let you know."

Dolly rested her elbows on the bar. The bartender came down to her. "Another drink, miss?"

"No."

When he went back to the end of the bar, she said, "I saw your name in the *Star-Invocation* this morning. Violet Solomon."

"Mr. Earnshaw's latest opinion piece." Violet said. "He must have been in a good mood. He only called me a 'dissolute temptress.' Last time it was 'vicious negress of dubious intelligence,' although he didn't use my name that time."

"He's quite an admirer."

"Oh, yes."

"Does he know his daughter drinks here?"

Violet sighed. "Suspects at least. But I've made sure I'm well connected and protected, even from him. As well as I can be, anyway."

"What about your bartender?"

"Him and Gabe, you mean?"

"No. I mean—" Dolly made a swoop under each eye with her index finger.

"Ah. Was that the rest of Mr. Earnshaw's editorial? Shape-shifters? I stopped reading."

"Some wolf family he's accused of criminal doings. He doesn't like shifters, that's for sure."

"Philippe's careful about where he changes. Other than that . . ." She shrugged and shook her head. "Oh. I see someone I should talk to." She dropped off the stool and strode through the crowd.

Dolly watched the bartender for a few minutes. He sensed her glance and looked up then came down without her beckoning. "Another one now, miss?"

"No. A favor. Will you hold on to a package for me?"

"Behind the bar, you mean?"

She shook her head. "Not here. I know Violet's careful, but speakeasies get raided. No, with you. It's small, about the size of a personal ledger."

"I s'pose I could."

"It'd be you. Not your sister, not the tattooist. You alone."

Was that a smile? He nodded. "Sure."

"If something happens to me, open it. You and your sister will know right away what it is. I'll pay you twenty-five cents a day."

"It must be important."

"Just some insurance. I'll bring it by the next time I come." She slid a quarter across the bar, a tip. "See you soon."

~

"What were you and Dolly White talking about last night?"

Philippe watched his sister make up Gabriel's plate, hoping she would forget the question. He didn't want to lie to his sister, but he'd promised Dolly White he wouldn't tell anyone about their deal.

Violet put the Spanish ham at twelve o'clock, the greens at six, and the rice at three. "Well?"

"Just talking," he said, leaning over to inhale the aroma of his own plate. Aunt Lily had made this, and it was one of his favorites. Violet often couldn't find the ham, but when she did, hers was almost as good.

"She's an interesting one." Gabriel tasted the rice and sighed. "Delicious."

"Thanks." Violet sat down. "You be careful, brother."

"Why? Like Gabriel said. She's interesting, that's all."

"Should I be worried?" Gabriel's expression was serious, but there was laughter in his voice.

"'Course not."

"Yeah . . ." Violet chewed thoughtfully. "She's as sharp as a sliver of glass, that one, and she'll cut you just as fast. That's what I hear."

"*You're* working with her." Sometimes his sister didn't make sense. It was safe enough for *her* to help the woman out; why couldn't he make some cash that same way?

Violet drifted her fork through the grains of rice. "She's paying. And she's making a run at the Earnshaws. Francis Earnshaw will never swing for what he and his gang did to Pedro. Anyone who pokes him where it hurts is all right in my book. But that doesn't mean I want *you* in the middle. The White King doesn't care whose blood he leaves on the floor, long as it's not his family. And you're a shape-shifter."

Philippe shrugged.

"She leaves people behind, Dolly does," Violet said. "That's what I hear."

"Grifters." Gabriel took a swallow of beer. "They all do. It's just how the job goes."

"Doesn't make it right," Violet said, "ever. You"—she pointed her fork at Philippe—"you be careful."

"You're just mad because the White King took a swipe at you in the papers again."

"Yeah, in the same article with the Doucette family. I have a right to be insulted."

"He doesn't name just the Doucettes, though, does he? He paints all the shape-shifters with the same brush." Gabriel folded his hands. "I'm starting to see the pattern." He looked worried.

"What pattern?" Violet said. "A week ago you said you didn't understand it."

"He can't prove the Doucettes are shim runners, because they're too well connected. But he can poison the well by calling them out as shifters. And they're getting squeezed by this Eastside gang, I hear."

"You hear everything," Philippe said. He longed to run his fingers through Gabriel's braids but kept his hands flat on the table.

"I do hear a lot. It's getting bad. There've been a couple of knifings on Queen Anne Hill, your old neighborhood, Violet. And a shooting."

"The Eastside gang must be connected too," Philippe said.

Violet shook her head. "I know what's going to happen. First they'll pass a curfew for shape-shifters, and they'll say, 'It's for your protection.' The Commission'll get involved, and pretty soon there'll be *laws* against shape-shifters."

"Whoa, Violet!" Philippe held up both hands, laughing. "Settle down! Nobody's doing that yet."

"That is how it goes, though. Usually," Gabriel said.

Philippe's stomach turned over. "They can't *outlaw* us, can they?"

"Can't they?" Violet said, glaring at Philippe as though it were all his fault. "You be careful. You be *extra* careful out there."

~

OCTOBER 23, 1929

(THREE WEEKS BEFORE)

Dolly made her way down the narrow stairs into the speakeasy. Violet's piano player played bluesy ragtime, and a blond girl in a fringed evening shift whirled and danced by herself.

"Gin?" the bartender said.

"Champagne." She seated herself at the bar. "Start me a tab, please."

"Sure thing, miss."

When he returned with a shallow glass twinkling with bubbles, she slid the slim, wrapped package across to him, two dollars on top of it. "In advance," she said.

He nodded and turned away, putting the parcel under his jacket.

Dolly turned in her chair, studying the room. Only the blond girl was dancing. Couples huddled together over the tables or in the velvet-upholstered booths, and a group of men stood in one corner across from the door. Violet herself moved around the room, stopping at each table to chat. When she saw Dolly, she came up to the bar. The hazy mirror behind it cast ovals of gold onto her dark skin and gave her black eyes a velvety look, like a pansy petal. "I've told Lazlo Penske to expect you," she said. "He's difficult, and he's expensive but the best around for special orders. There's something he wants you to see."

"Is that usual?"

"I don't know. If he knocks down his price a bit, it's a good thing for you."

Dolly nodded her thanks and looked at the dancing girl. "Is that Fiona Earnshaw?"

"That's her." Violet raised a hand to two newcomers.

"Is it wise to let her stay?"

Violet watched the girl. "It's handy to know what the White King is up to. I've got family to protect, among other things."

Dolly lifted the glass to her lips without drinking. It didn't take hard work to draw a line between the Order of Saint Michael and the waterfront fire two years ago, but she had no need to press Violet about it. She looked back at the dancing girl. "There are rumors, you know, that she has a shimmershim problem."

Violet nodded. "I've told her to stop bringing it here, but

I know the signs. And if she takes a shot outside before she comes in . . ." She shrugged.

The song finished, and the girl staggered back to a booth in the corner.

Dolly beckoned to the bartender and slid over a sawbuck. "The bottle, please, and another glass."

He complied. She drained her glass, then, holding the bottle by the neck, the glasses in her other hand, walked over to the booth.

The blond girl looked up. Her pupils were nearly invisible in irises like scraps of the summer sky. "Bubbly!" she said. She waved her hand over her head. "Philippe! Is it the good stuff?"

Dolly glanced over her shoulder to see the bartender nod.

Fiona lowered her hand. "Who're you?"

Dolly slipped into the booth and poured a glass of champagne. "I'd cut back on the gin if I were you. With the shim, you're giving your liver a death sentence."

"Oh, a Samaritan," the girl said. "What's your name?"

"Dolly White."

"I don't know you, do I?"

"No, but I know you."

Fiona shook her head, the yellow light flaring off her pale bob. "Everybody knows us. My father is Ambrose Earnshaw, Commissioner of Magi. My brother is Francis Earnshaw. *Semper Servo* and all that." The girl held out her hands, palms up. "Ladies and gentlemen, meet magicless Fiona, runt of the litter."

Dolly pushed the shallow champagne glass forward, using the back of her hand to nudge the gin glass out of Fiona's reach. "I hear you're getting married."

"I heard that too," Fiona said.

"It's not to your liking?"

Animation left Fiona's pretty face, and except for those eyes, she looked sober. "Tony's fine."

"But there's someone else. Someone you love."

"There was."

It could have been said with bitterness, but the last word, instead, rang with the hollowness of loss. Some gesture was called for. She touched Fiona's hand briefly. "Tell me," she said.

Fiona looked down at the table. "His name is Rob. Magicless. There is no problem with his pedigree, but Daddy—" She reached for the empty champagne glass. Dolly poured in a splash. "Daddy has other plans."

"Defy Daddy. You have money, don't you?"

Fiona shook her head. "I did. My grandfather—Mama's father—left me money in a trust, to come to me when I turned twenty-five. The executor died two years ago, and Daddy got control of the money." She sniffed and rubbed her nose with the back of her hand.

"What would you do if you had money?"

"Of my own, you mean? I'd leave the house. I'd marry Rob, if he'd have me." She sniffed again. "I'd run away if I could, but even Mama's jewels are locked up in Daddy's vault."

"Vaults can be opened."

"The vault's blood-magicked," Fiona said, the confirmation Dolly expected.

"Well." Dolly folded her hands on the table, about an inch away from Fiona's. "That just makes it challenging."

Now Fiona did look up. "You're a thief."

"I am that."

"You want to steal something from Daddy."

Dolly smiled and nodded.

"Do you . . . do you think you would help me?"

Dolly looked thoughtful. "I'd need someone I could depend on. With the shim . . ." She shook her head. "If you could give it up . . . Could you go for four days without a slug of it?"

Fiona's eyes widened, but she considered the question. Her head bobbed in a quick nod.

Dolly smiled more broadly. "Fiona, I think we can help each other."

Chapter Seven

OCTOBER 27, 1929

(THREE WEEKS BEFORE)

THE FOG CARRIED A metallic smell above the brine of Elliott Bay. Dolly's steps plonked on the wharf. She watched and listened. This was a neighborhood of unlicensed magickers, subject to random sweeps by the police and the midnight punishments of the Order of Saint Michael. They were wary of outsiders.

The daily newspaper carried a front-page picture of a ruined roadster, owned by Miss Fiona Earnshaw. Miss Earnshaw had been unharmed. A rain-slicked road was given as the cause. This accident was a bad turn of events, if the girl had so little control.

Penske's Kitchen Herbs sat close to the end of the pier, one dim electric light glowing above the door. The tiny bell fixed above it chimed as she went in.

Light seeped out from the open arch behind the counter. She inhaled the scents of thyme, fish, cedar, and smoke. Bundles of dried plants hung from the ceiling, and the long bins stretching the length of the room were filled with crushed dried leaves and flowers.

A man came through the arch. He was taller than her, with a fringe of fine black hair circling a shining bald spot. He walked with a bit of a stoop and wheezed slightly. "We're closed. Come back tomorrow, lady," he said.

"Violet Solomon recommended you," she said. "I'm having a dinner party. Very exclusive. She said you have the best fresh herbs."

He stepped forward and rested his hands on the counter, his breathing labored. His gaze was both intense and distant, as if he stared through her into something she could not see. He was filled with fatigue or grief. She could not always distinguish those two.

He held out one hand palm up and twitched his fingers. She handed him her list.

"Paean's Touch," he said.

She nodded.

"Oblivion powder, bladders of spider web, a bone needle, preservation vials . . ." He glanced up. "Blood magic. This must be *very* exclusive."

She didn't bother to respond.

"You're the one from San Francisco," he said. "Your . . . dinner parties are the best, Violet says."

Dolly's job in San Francisco had been a spectacular failure, and the client she had disappointed was notorious for punishing those who failed him.

"Oh, the last one was a complete fiasco," she said cheerfully. "But I'm optimistic about this next one. If I can get the right ingredients."

She waited while he considered. He looked up at her again, and the distance left his gaze as he studied her.

"Did she tell you the price, that Violet?"

"She said there was something you wanted me to see."

"Yes." His voice roughened, and his eyes had a sheen she

didn't like. But she needed the best.

Since she fled San Francisco, she had spent months researching and preparing for the Earnshaw job. Violet had come through with the greengrocer, and Fiona was all lined up, but Dolly needed the best tools. The whole job could have derailed with Fiona's car crash. Could the girl even carry out her part, if it really meant giving up shim? Involving her was a risk Dolly was starting to question.

She needed Penske badly. And she could only hope he didn't realize it.

"Lead the way," she said, and followed him through the arch into the back room. As she had guessed, it was filled with amulets, blessed medallions, and other charms. There were delicate protective amulets of silver and the government-issue steel and onyx bands soldiers had used during the war. Penske had magical vessels and alembics and a flat of magical herbs. They went out the back door and along a narrow wharf. He started down a flight of stairs marked with light reflecting off the water.

As she looked at the rippling steps, a memory overtook her of a long fall into a twilit place.

She forced herself to step down.

Next to a thick masonry wall, Penske led her lower, along a shallow flight of steps. She would hear the soughing of the waves above her. It was cold here, and dark.

She looked around. "Where are you taking me?"

"Why? Are you afraid the fairies will steal you?"

"Not anymore," she said.

"You sound like you've visited them already."

"I did."

"Really?" His voice echoed a bit. "What did they give you?"

"A nose for magic," she said. "No *gift* for it, but an ability to recognize it and recognize charlatans."

"And what did they take from you?"

The stairs ended, and she stepped onto a thin layer of mud. She didn't bother to answer. The darkness was not uniform; buildings blocked out the stars. Penske stopped at one of them.

He unlocked the door, and she followed him in. It was some kind of warehouse. The first room was bare. Penske walked across it to a set of double doors that coasted back when he pushed them. Cold air rolled out, condensing into a silvery mist as she watched. He disappeared inside. After a moment she stepped into the mist.

It had a familiar smell: ice.

Two small jewel-toned lanterns lit the room. At first glance, it seemed as if a woman floated in midair, her black hair spread around her head like a rayed crown, her feet pointed, her hands crossed on her chest. A white silk cloth draped her body.

Dolly took a breath and came into the room. The woman was not floating. She was frozen in ice so transparent Dolly could only find the smoothed edges of the block by the glancing of the light.

Penske stood at the foot of the block. She understood his wheezing now; an air elemental was breathing him. Air elementals were the most dangerous elementals because they were the most curious about humans. In return for breathing him, *knowing* him, the creature was keeping the ice frozen. "Your daughter?"

"My niece, Sofia," he said. "My sister's child. Dead five days."

"Did she drown?"

He shot her a look of incandescent anger. "Take a look. Tell me how she died."

She moved up to the edge of the ice block and peered down. The woman seemed twenty-two or-three, a couple of years older than Fiona. Her skin was pale except for the purple lines marking her neck. "Someone strangled her."

"Yes." She heard the roughness of his breath. "Someone strangled her."

"I'm not a detective, Mr. Penske. Far from it."

"I don't need a detective. I need vengeance."

"I can't avenge her."

"Look at her! All she did, to earn this death, was say no. Because of who he is, there will never be justice for her. This could be you."

In fact, in height, in the shape of the face and the shoulders, the hair, it *could* be her.

Her current job was work enough. She couldn't split her attention to track down another wealthy man, find his weakness, and puncture him, no matter how much she needed Penske. And she had promised her client in Wichita a void mask. She could not spare the time, not now.

"She drew an attractive man into her light, and he killed her," she said. "If I cried for every woman that happened to, Mr. Penske, I'd cry every day. You must know who did this."

"We know," he said.

"There's no evidence?"

"While someone choked the life out of her, *he* was with his friends at a supper club. They all swore it. His notes to her, ones filled at first with poetry and later with threats, caught fire in my sister's desk when no one was present and burned to ash. There is only one thing, a blessed medallion. She tore it from his neck. She scratched him. His skin was under her nails."

"So you have his essence," she pointed out.

Penske shook his head. "She lay hidden for *three days.* Even a preservation vial could not restore his essence." He reached into his pocket and drew out a scrap of red silk. "The price for *my* help is *your* help. Avenge my niece."

"My guest list's already pretty full," she said.

He held the silk out to her. She didn't want to touch it, to look at it, but in this room, pinned under his gaze, she didn't dare refuse. She took the cloth and flipped it back. The medallion was commonplace: Saint Michael, sword raised in his right hand. *Semper Servo.* Always Protect.

She flipped it over, tilted it to the light to read the engraving. FAE.

"Oh," she said. "Francis Ambrose Earnshaw?"

"Yes."

"I see." She looked at the frozen woman. Her plan came together, and with it a way to leave her San Francisco troubles behind her for good—not a trail merely grown cold, a trail dead-ended. "All right, Mr. Penske. You are definitely on my guest list."

~

NOVEMBER 11, 1929

(SIX DAYS BEFORE)

She glanced again at her wristwatch. Her left foot swung in a circle, and she consciously made it stop. "The art museum closes at four. Earnshaw will have questions if I'm not back soon after that." Her throat was scratchy.

"I can give you something for the fear," Penske said. The room was as cold as before. Inside the salt circle, she worked hard to keep from shivering.

"I don't need anything," she said.

She had brought him what she had written of the spell Earnshaw had recited her first day in the house, the one that opened the door to her. "It's a bell jar lock," Penske said. "Basic, but your counterspell must be exact, and once it is spoken, *you* must be the one to open the door, or the counterspell fails." Dolly had some experience with word magic, but the bell jar counterspell was ceremonial, and there were gestures that had to be performed at exactly the right moment. Penske had rehearsed her for an hour, and now she was hoarse and tired. It was never good to be tired when dealing with an elemental.

He nodded but still stood, arms folded, looking at her.

She felt an unusual rush of anger. "Are you getting cold feet?" she said. "Does this somehow besmirch your niece's memory? You're the one who wanted vengeance."

"No," he said, but she heard the hesitation. "Sofia is no longer here, and this should not besmirch her memory. I'm wondering if you are strong enough."

"I am that," she said.

He gave a half shrug and turned away. She made herself breathe slowly and deeply.

Penske spoke the summoning, the words in a language she did not recognize rushing and whistling like the wind through a crack in the wall.

The room grew still, and then the elemental was with her, within the circle. It was a being of air, and she could not see it exactly, but she felt its scrutiny. Again, purposefully, she regulated her breathing.

The airy thing drew closer, and her chest grew tighter. As Penske had instructed her, she gazed straight ahead, blinking as she needed to. The air around her face grew cooler, colder, and colder still.

Every pore in her face, neck, and hands erupted in prickles. The thing pushed deeper; her nostrils and throat burned with cold. Deeper, and it breathed her, glacially cold. She tried to stay calm, but it felt like a bellows was forcing snow into her lungs.

It could not get worse, yet somehow it did. It could not go on any longer, but somehow it did. Then it ended. Her whole body shook, and she slumped against the chair back. The air she inhaled was warm, and she sucked it in greedily.

"Are you all right?" Penske smudged aside the salt barrier and held out a cup. She started to reach for it, but her hand shook too badly. He held it to her lips. She took three swallows, and the sweetness of the warm brew strengthened her.

She heard a sighing sound behind them and a sharp crack. She started. "What was that?"

"Come look."

She stood up hesitantly. Strength trickled back into her legs, and she walked over to the block of ice.

The clear ice had grown white and frosty, and a crack ran the length of the block, where the air elemental had made its way in. She stared at the face of the woman frozen inside. The green eyes, the forehead, the cheekbones, the shape of the lips . . . She saw them every time she looked in the mirror. The elemental, having gone into her and taking onto itself the shape of her face, had laid it over the dead woman's.

"How long?"

Penske said, "She'll be safely buried before the illusion leaves her."

She didn't ask him what the price was. His breathing had grown even rougher. The elemental would breathe him until he died, probably.

He stared down at the woman, his hands clenched on the block of ice. A faint sound came from his throat, nearly a moan. Or a sob. He whispered something he couldn't quite make out, but it might have been *gone.*

"It's a good likeness," she said.

"A perfect likeness," said Penske.

"Are you prepared for this? If you're not, Mr. Penske, tell me now."

He looked up, startled. Then his lip lifted in a sneer. "Of *course* I am ready."

"She'll need the clothes. Are you prepared for that?"

"My sister is, and she will help."

"Your sister . . . her mother? Is that wise?"

He glared. "We have already held a rosary for her. We all know this—*this* is not Sofia."

"All right," Dolly said, "but the trickiest part is still ahead."

PART THREE

CHANGELING

Chapter Eight

NOVEMBER 14, 1929

(THREE DAYS BEFORE)

DOLLY WOKE THE NEXT morning with her neck aching dully. Francis's fingers had left lavender bruises. She applied some arnica lotion and draped a light scarf around her neck. She and Fiona shared breakfast and went out for a walk. The sky was a clear blue, and the breeze was cold. They headed for Volunteer Park.

A blue sedan sat parked at one of the intersections. Three men sat inside. Fiona peered in before Dolly could stop her. "Good morning, Henry!" she said.

The man in the back turned his head away and said nothing.

Fiona stopped, her hands on her hips, but Dolly slipped one arm through hers and pulled the girl away. "What are you doing?"

"What is *he* doing? Did you see that? He just snubbed me! He's a great friend of Francis, he's at the house often, but he snubs me on a street corner? Wait till I tell Francis."

"Maybe it would be better if you didn't."

"Why not? And what are they doing out here, anyway, just sitting, this time of morning?"

"I don't think we want the answer to that question," Dolly said, scanning the streets ahead. On the next block, across the road, two roughly dressed men had backed a third one up against a picket fence. She couldn't see the third man's face, but his height and the color of his skin were clear from where they stood.

"Let's go—" She started to draw Fiona back, but the girl had already seen.

"What are they doing?" She pulled free and started up the sidewalk.

"Fiona."

The third man had a wheelbarrow, and now the two men kicked it over. Carrots spilled onto the sidewalk, and a pair of cabbages rolled into the street.

"That's not right." Fiona walked faster. She took Dolly by surprise and got several feet ahead before Dolly caught up with her.

"It's not our concern."

"Don't you know who that is? That's—"

"He's Mrs. Chambers's bootlegger."

"He's Violet's bartender!"

"He can handle himself, Fiona. Come on, we'll turn down this block."

"Dolly—" Fiona shook her head. She darted into the street, heading for the altercation.

Curse the girl. Dolly followed, nearly running. She grabbed Fiona's arm.

"Don't try to stop me."

"Follow me," Dolly said, pushing Fiona behind her. She could see Philippe's face clearly now. One of the men moved closer and held up his arm. It didn't look like a pending blow, more as if he were going to press the back of his hand against Philippe's forehead. Gold and blue shone on the man's wrist.

Philippe staggered against the fence, shaking his head. His eyes flashed a deep green, and his lips pulled back from his teeth.

Dolly raised her voice. "*There* he is! You've got him!" She trotted up to them. "Thank you, gentlemen!"

"This isn't your business, sister," the second man said.

The first man dropped his arm, pulling his cuff down over the gold-and-blue amulet he wore. Fiona's eyes widened as she stared at his wrist.

Dolly ignored the men and stepped close to Philippe, shaking her finger in his face. "You! How dare you! Do you think we'd eat that lettuce? It was filled with earwigs! *Crawling* with them! You come back to the house right now and you give Mrs. Chambers back her money!"

"I'm not—" Fiona's voice shook, but she steadied it. "I'm not eating bugs for lunch. You should be ashamed."

"I—I'm sorry, miss. I only deliver—" Philippe looked down at the ground. His shoulders rippled, and he panted.

"This isn't your business," the second man said again.

"It is. Mrs. Chambers sent us after him," Dolly said. "Thank *goodness* you two were here to stop him! You, pick up that mess and right your cart. You're coming back with us now."

"We don't care about bad lettuce," the first man said. "This negro is a criminal. He's a bootlegger."

"Oh?" Dolly glanced at the man, looking surprised, then whipped back around on Philippe. "Don't think you can skulk away! Pick up that barrow!"

"Yes, miss." Philippe pulled away from the second man and stooped to turn over the wheelbarrow.

"Where does he hide his spirits?" Fiona said. "I don't see any."

It was a risk, though Dolly admired Fiona's nerve. There were no bottles on the pavement or in the wheelbarrow.

"He's already made all his deliveries for today." The second man put his hands on his hips. "He's got dirty money in his pockets, and you two girls don't want to know what *else* he's capable of."

The blue sedan drove past. The first man watched it go.

"He's certainly capable of cheating our cook," Dolly said, putting *her* hands on her hips now. "I doubt Mr. Ambrose Earnshaw will be pleased about this!"

"Forget it, Lou. The cook needs her money back." The first man reached out and nudged Philippe's leg with his foot, hard. "This boy's a coward, he won't try anything." He turned away.

The second man looked startled then glared at Dolly. "Suit yourself, sister." He followed.

Fiona bent down to pick up a cabbage.

"Don't help me, Miss Fiona," Philippe said. She straightened back up, her hands clasped tightly.

They waited while he put the ruined vegetables into the barrow. "I don't know why they were on me, miss, but I could have handled it," he said, not meeting Dolly's eyes.

"You could *not* have. Don't you read the papers?"

Philippe tossed the last half-flattened cabbage head into the barrow and started back the way he had come. "It's a good thing I'd made my deliveries. They wanted my money, that's all. It's not the first time I've been jumped. And there were only two of them."

"There weren't two."

"Yes, there were," Fiona said.

"There were five."

"Five? You mean, Henry?" Fiona stopped walking. "What

are you saying?"

"I'm saying they were waiting. They're part of the Order of Saint Michael, aren't they?"

"Well, yes, but the Order doesn't care about bootleggers."

"They care about shape-shifters, apparently. Didn't you see the lapis lazuli amulet that thug had on his wrist?"

Philippe gave her a wide-eyed glance.

"Dolly!" Fiona said. "You shouldn't just accuse people!"

"Look at those marks on his face, Fiona."

"I—" Fiona turned and stared at Philippe. "*Are* you? Is Violet—"

"Just me, Miss Fiona."

"Are you a wolf?"

"No, Miss Fiona. I'm a man. When I change I'm a puma . . . a cougar. I don't change in the city. I don't attack people. At least, I wouldn't without a reason."

"Fiona, we need to keep moving," Dolly said.

"I never . . ." Fiona said. "I never knew."

"Of course not, because he controls it. All shifters do." Dolly stared at Philippe. "You even managed to control it when he used a shifter stone on you. How did you do that?"

"I barely did. I think . . . A friend gave me a protection tattoo. I think it helped ward the shifter-stone just enough."

The tattooist. She glanced up and down the street. "You'd better change your route for a while. You'd be better off close to home until whatever this is blows over."

"I'll go now. Thank you for helping me."

"Thank Fiona. It was her idea."

He looked up. "Thank you, Miss Fiona."

Fiona was squeezing her hands together. "I didn't really do anything."

He nodded and pushed the wheelbarrow down the street.

Dolly gave Fiona a quick glance. "I'll catch up with you," she said.

Philippe stopped. She hurried up to him. "Would you like some extra cash?" she said quietly. "It's a job."

He fiddled with the handle of the wheelbarrow. "The Earnshaws?"

He owed her; she took the risk. "Yes. I need someone who knows the neighborhood and doesn't get rattled." She whispered a couple of quick sentences. Would he back off when he heard what she needed?

He studied her. "Will this take out the son?"

She nodded again.

"I'm in," he said.

"I mean it now. You be careful," she said loudly, turning her back on him.

Fiona's face was pale. "I didn't know. I didn't know he was . . . How could I?"

"You wouldn't have." Dolly touched the girl's shoulder. "Let's get back to the house. You need to tell Mrs. Chambers what happened."

"Why? She'll just be embarrassed."

Dolly spoke slowly. "So she'll know what to say if she's asked about it."

"Daddy won't ask. He doesn't care." She caught her breath. "Oh. The lettuce."

"That's right."

They continued walking.

"How did you know about those marks? I never . . . his skin's so dark, I thought they were just scars."

"On the East Coast they're called shifter's marks. Quite

popular. Leopard spots."

"Back east?"

"I have friends in New York and other places. They aren't so hateful about shape-shifters other places as they are here. They're just considered magickers like everyone else. One I know is a war hero." She let herself think back, for just a moment, to the detective in San Francisco, the wolf who had busted up her San Francisco grift and brought down a circle of German spies in the process.

"And lapis lazuli, that's a shifter stone? That blue-and-gold amulet? It can force someone to shift?"

"Usually, yes." Dolly walked a few more paces. "You look like you recognized it."

"Not that one, one like it. Daddy had a pair like that. The Commission used them."

Dolly kept her voice neutral. "I'm sure they did."

"I didn't know what they were for." Fiona walked seven steps. "Did . . . do you think someone used one on that wolf-girl in the market?"

"It seems likely."

"You know a lot, Dolly."

"I studied."

"Why do you do . . . what you do? I mean, you could teach or write books or be a magus's assistant."

"I'm good at what I do. Don't you think people should do what they're good at?"

Fiona shrugged. It wasn't just the question that was flummoxing her, Dolly thought, it was the whole morning. They were both quiet as they made their way back to the house.

~

As he sat down at the dinner table, Earnshaw glanced at the scarf around her neck and then away. Dolly looked at Earnshaw, remembering how he had boasted of hearing everything that went on in his house.

"I expect the Commission meeting to run long tonight," he said. "I'm holding their feet to the fire about this Penske fellow."

Fiona and Francis both nodded. He looked at each of them, preening his mustache with thumb and forefinger. "Fiona, I heard from Mrs. Arbelio today. It sounds as if the party planning is progressing, and she is very pleased."

"I hope so," Fiona said. "Francis, what did you do to your neck?"

"Cut myself shaving," he said. He turned to Dolly. "Remind me. You took care of Mortimer's aunt, in California?"

"Miss Minerva was actually his mother's aunt," she said.

"Some dainty old lady with cats, I guess."

"I wouldn't call her dainty," she said. "She grew up in California when it was still part of the frontier. And no cats. She had a very old and smelly bird-hunting dog, some sort of spaniel." She looked at Earnshaw. "A king's name. King James?"

"A King Charles spaniel," Earnshaw said.

"Yes. I think she and the dog both missed hunting dreadfully."

"Why are we talking about some dead relative of Uncle Mort?" Fiona said. "You aren't patrolling tonight, are you, Francis?"

"Why? I'm surprised you're interested."

"You're not wearing your medallion, and you've been getting home later and later. I worry."

Francis stared at her. "I believe you do." He raised his wineglass. "Baby Sister is truly back among us! A toast!"

They raised their glasses. "To success," Earnshaw said.

"Take care," said Fiona.

"Yes," Dolly said, giving Francis a sideways glance. "Take care. Seattle can be dangerous."

~

The next day Dolly met Tony Arbelio and his mother for the first time. After Inez served them a light lunch, Mrs. Arbelio took over the small parlor, quizzing Fiona over the particulars of the engagement party.

Tony was mostly quiet. He was as tall as Francis, with curly black hair and dark eyes. His nose was too long for him to be considered handsome, but he was attractive. When he got a word in, he was witty without being mean. Dolly thought he and Fiona could easily come to an arrangement and create a perfectly respectable society marriage if they chose to. She thought of Loughlin's comment about the clubs. For the Arbelio scion, marriage would probably be like walking every day in a pair of shoes one size too small.

Fiona answered each question calmly, and Dolly watched as Mrs. Arbelio's posture changed from the forward lean of a woman poised to swoop in and set things straight to a more relaxed, upright pose. Her responses expanded from brisk nods to one-or two-word comments of approval. Tony looked a bit surprised and stared into his lemonade when he saw Dolly watching him.

Earnshaw came in just as they were finishing up. "How does it all look, Olivia?"

"It will do, Ambrose. The hotel, modern, as you know, but

quite acceptable. Their chef is excellent. I've checked. The theme, the decorations, lovely."

"I'm glad. Give Vincent my regards."

They walked the Arbelios to the door. Fiona went out with them to have a few private words with Tony. Earnshaw turned to Dolly. "You've done very well. Olivia is a taskmaster. If she approves, things must indeed be excellent."

"It's Fiona's doing," Dolly said. "She has a flair for organization."

Earnshaw nodded. "A good trait in a wife," he said.

~

Someone tapped on her door. Dolly looked up from her journal. It was a bit difficult to write, because there was still a streak of numbness in her right hand.

"Dolly, may I come in?" Fiona said.

"Of course."

Before she could stand, Fiona came in. She closed the door and leaned against it. "I thought you should know. Uncle Mort is here."

For a second Dolly didn't understand what Fiona meant. "Oh!" she said. She let her voice sound warm. "Mr. Lester. Do you know we've never met in person?" She wondered why he was here. "I sent him a thank-you letter, but I certainly should express my gratitude in person."

"Oh, well. Good." Fiona looked at the journal. "Is that Chinese?"

Dolly laughed. "No. It's a form of stenographic writing. Much faster than cursive. Miss Meritage taught it to us."

Fiona's brow wrinkled. She sat down on Dolly's bed.

"Wouldn't you hate being a stenographer?"

"I think I would. But it's good to have skills. Is Mr. Lester staying for dinner, do you think?"

"I don't think so. His visit's unexpected. I wanted you to know . . . I didn't know if it would be awkward."

Dolly had searched the room high and low every few days, looking for a hidden earshot gemstone. She'd never found one, but she and Fiona had agreed to act as if any conversation inside the house was being overheard. She didn't think Earnshaw cared enough to plant an earshot gem in her room, but his firstborn was another matter. Francis would use any advantage.

"Not awkward at all. He just dropped by? I didn't think gentlemen did that." She wondered if she needed to give Lester some encouragement to keep her secret.

"Not usually." Fiona looked at the sock doll on Dolly's bed. "What is this? Did you make it?

"I did. The first thing all of us learned at Miss Meritage's was how to knit, and we each made a sock doll. Most of Miss Meritage's girls carry them everywhere. A keepsake, I suppose you'd say."

"Is she you? She's got green eyes, hasn't she?"

Dolly shrugged.

"And this skirt! So colorful, it's like something from a circus."

"We had a huge ragbag in the laundry room. I made her skirt from those. Those of us with no magical abilities sewed quilts or wove rag rugs when we weren't in class."

"You weaving rugs." Fiona stroked the strips of cloth. "I can't picture it." She reached for the doll.

Dolly stood at once and smoothed the front of her skirt.

She touched her hair. "Shall we go down? I'd hate to miss Mr. Lester."

Fiona hopped off the bed. "Yes, let's. I've asked Inez to serve coffee in the drawing room." At the door, she turned. "Since you haven't met him before, I will say... Just, mind him, Dolly."

"Mind him?"

"You'll know."

Inez followed them into the drawing room and laid out the coffee service. They sat on the sofa. Dolly raised her eyebrows as a man's voice, high and agitated, sounded through the closed door of the study.

"Oh, my," Fiona said. "Uncle Mort must be really upset."

"Is he excitable? He never seemed to be, on the telephone."

"I've never heard him raise his voice except at baseball games."

"... Doucette ..." The one word carried to them clearly.

"Well, business is tense these days after the stock market crash." Dolly folded her hands in her lap.

"Uncle Mort was *mostly* in East-side real estate," Fiona said, but she sounded doubtful.

"... do you *mean*, they won't act without ..."

Earnshaw's voice, a single barked word, overrode Lester. The study grew quiet.

"I feel like I'm eavesdropping." Fiona gave a short, high-pitched laugh.

"Nonsense. We're in a completely different room with a closed door between us and them."

Fiona fidgeted and put her hand on her throat.

Dolly shifted her position a little and raised her voice. "I'm so *glad* Mrs. Arbelio approved our plans. If we had to redo everything, just as we're getting ready to send out invitations, that would have been a disaster."

"Oh, yes. Yes." Fiona stopped just short of shouting. "Such a relief. She can be quite set in her opinions."

"Shall we have coffee?"

"Oh, no. Let's wait for Daddy and Uncle Mort."

They waited, looking at each other. A few moments later, the door opened. Earnshaw spoke over his shoulder. "I can't just *make* something happen, Mort."

A man answered from inside the study. "I disagree." Dolly recognized Francis's voice.

Earnshaw stepped out of his study. Lester came out behind him, his face the dull red shade Dolly knew well. "The Commission would feel differently if wolves were rampaging through *their* neighborhoods!"

"It's not your neighborhood." Earnshaw stood on the threshold of the drawing room.

"My tenants—"

"Mort."

Fiona stood up, and after a second Dolly did too. Earnshaw led the way into the room, and Lester followed. He stopped when he saw Dolly. Francis bumped into him.

"Uncle Mort!" Fiona held out her hand. "This is a pleasant surprise."

He ignored her hand and stepped around Earnshaw. "Fiona, you look radiant." He kissed her cheek and wrapped his arms around her. Fiona giggled and a second later wiggled free.

Dolly extended her hand, keeping the coffee table between them. "Mr. Lester, we've never met in person. I'm Dolly White."

"I—Yes." He gripped her hand and dropped it.

Behind him, Francis narrowed his eyes. His glance lit on Dolly and flicked back to Lester.

"Thank you so much for recommending me for this position."

"Yes, Mort, I'd give you a bottle of aged scotch, if it were legal," Earnshaw said, dropping into his chair in the corner. Fiona stepped out of Lester's reach and went around. She poured coffee into a cup and carried it to her father.

"Francis?"

"None for me. Let me get this straight. You never actually *met* Dolly, Mort? But you sent her to our house."

"We spoke on the phone. On several occasions. Several. And Aunt Minerva spoke highly of Miss White."

"And I'm glad you did recommend her," Fiona said. She came back around and sat down. She poured a coffee for herself. "She's been so helpful. You can't imagine, Uncle Mort, how nice it is to have another woman to talk to sometimes. Especially in *this* house, where it's business, business, business all the time."

Earnshaw let out one of his roaring laughs. "Is that your gentle way of saying we were too loud, Fiona? Emotions run high when people's safety is at risk."

"Safety?" Dolly sat back down and folded her hands.

Francis sat in the chair to the left of the sofa. She did not look at him, but she could tell he was watching her. She kept her gaze on Earnshaw.

"Wolves. Shape-shifters." Lester still sounded flustered. He looked around then took the seat across the table from Fiona.

"No more shoptalk." Earnshaw sipped his coffee. He looked at Lester, who hunched his shoulders.

"Coffee, Mr. Lester?" Dolly reached for the pot.

"No, I . . . Well, yes."

"Cream? Sugar?"

"Two sugars."

She added sugar to his coffee and handed the saucer and cup across the table to him. He sipped so loudly that she could hear it, and Fiona frowned.

"So, what did you two talk about, on those telephone calls?" Francis said.

"Usually about Miss Minerva and how she was doing," Dolly said before Lester could speak.

"Yes. And Aunt Minerva wrote to me. Regularly."

"Still, it seems . . . odd. Don't you think?"

Dolly looked down at her lap. "I'll confess, I reached out to Mr. Lester when I came to Seattle. It was a bit . . . unconventional, I know."

"I explored Dolly's background thoroughly," Earnshaw said. "She has good recommendations from others. And you can't argue with the results."

"It's not like she's a secret unionist," Fiona said, "or a *bootlegger*."

There was a silence in the room. Fiona's choice had been inspired, reminding all the men of the place she had been frequenting only a few weeks ago.

Earnshaw chuckled. "Certainly not a unionist."

"I'm not even sure I know what that means." Dolly sipped her black coffee.

Fiona led the conversation from there, chattering like a society girl, drawing chuckles from her father and even one from Lester. Francis watched his sister with an expressionless face, shifting to study Lester and glance once or twice at Dolly, who tossed in a comment now and again.

"I bet Dolly could tell us some wonderful stories about Mort's aunt," Francis said, cutting across what Fiona had been saying. "Couldn't you, Dolly?"

"Great-aunt. And no, I couldn't possibly do Miss Minerva justice. Between the hunting dog—"

"The dog," Lester said, nodding.

"And the shotguns—"

"The shotguns."

"And all her tales of California after those gold rush years, you'll just have to take my word that she was a character."

"Force of nature," Lester said. He set down his cup and stood up. "I have to get going."

Fiona stood also, keeping the table between them, and held out her hand again. "Goodbye, Uncle Mort. We'll see you at the engagement party."

"I wouldn't miss it," he said. "I wonder if I might have a moment with Miss White?"

Fiona looked startled and glanced around the room. "Well, of course—"

Dolly skirted the table and went behind Francis's chair. "We can speak in the foyer, Mr. Lester."

He trailed her out. Francis followed them both and stood leaning against the wall.

Dolly went to the front door, opened it, and stepped outside. Lester followed and gripped her arm. "I need my ledger." He turned his head, glancing back at the house. "Now."

"It's safe. And it'll stay safe as long as long as I'm safe. Not a moment longer."

"Don't threaten me!"

"Don't threaten *me*, Mr. Lester." She glanced at the door and raised her voice. "I will never be able to repay you for this kindness."

The door opened. "Finished?" Francis said.

Lester flinched. "Just a question about something at Aunt Minerva's house," he said. "Miss White explained it to me."

"Did she?"

"So glad I could help," Dolly said, smiling and stepping back out of the reach of both men. Francis was becoming a problem. She needed to move quickly, but some of the timing was out of her control. It depended on so many other things.

And what was Lester up to?

Chapter Nine

NOVEMBER 15, 1929

(TWO DAYS BEFORE)

VIOLET DIDN'T KNOW ANYONE named Chambers, but she took the envelope and tipped the scruffy boy a nickel. Inside the envelope was another one, sealed, and inside it were five fresh five-dollar bills. She shoved the money into her pocket, locked up the bar's account book, closed the empty shop, and went down the street to Gabe's apartment. There was about an hour of daylight left, two days until whatever job it was Philippe had taken, the one he wouldn't tell her about.

Philippe had a key from the first week, but a year ago Gabe gave her one too. She always knocked, though, and waited for Gabe to invite her in. He wouldn't when he was working. This afternoon, he called her in.

"Dolly White pays her debts," she said. "I got my finder's fee."

He was rubbing down one of the needles with alcohol. He carried the case with him nearly everywhere now, since the fire. They gave Violet the willies.

"What's she getting my brother into? He won't tell me."

"So you think I should, Violet?" He said it gently.

"I'm worried. Do you blame me?"

He put the wooden needle in its spot in the leather case.

"No. 'Course not. I think she asked him to hold something for her. It seems like an insurance policy more than anything."

"Is it magic?"

Gabe shrugged. "I don't know."

She walked over and sat down across from him. "Do you know how much I want to go back home right now and rip through everything of his until I find it?"

He smiled now. "Yes, I do. And I know you won't. Because you know your brother is a man, not a little boy anymore."

"I know he isn't. I hate it. He leads with his heart, and I don't like it. That thing up there on Broadway the other morning. That *scared* me, Gabe."

"Well, Miss White and Miss Earnshaw helped him out of that jam."

"Last people he should be counting on. And where is he now? Right back up there making his deliveries."

Gabe nodded.

"They say she's a changeling. They say she worked for the Germans. The job in San Francisco? They say she worked for a German wizard."

"And they say she worked *against* the Germans during the war, for the Americans."

Violet chewed on her lower lip. She'd heard that too. "All that means is she'll work for anybody who pays her. Is she human? Does she have a heart?"

"That's the question."

Violet waited. "Well, Gabe? That *is* the question. Does she?"

"Oh, you're asking me?" Gabe shrugged. "I've got no idea. That's *her* question. That's the question the needles wanted to answer. They wanted to give her a heart."

"So she doesn't have one."

"It doesn't work that way. The needles answer the question, but you have to interpret the answer. A heart tattoo could mean you need a human heart. It could be a reminder that you already have one. The needles have their own language. I'm just their hands."

"I hate magic."

She sat, tapping her folded hands on the table while Gabe put each of his tools into its designated slot and rolled up the carrying case. "You'll come over for dinner?" she said finally.

"I will. One of my clients gave me a pineapple cake. I'll bring it along."

"That sounds good." She got up and made it nearly to the door. "Gabe? What else did she ask my brother to do?"

"What makes you think there was anything else?"

"Oh, come on, Gabe."

He turned in his chair. He tilted his face in her direction. "I can't tell you, Violet. Honestly can't."

She turned away.

"Violet?"

Against her judgment, she looked back.

"He doesn't tell me everything either," he said.

"Yeah." She yanked open the door. "Fine. Aren't we a pair of useless fools?"

~

NOVEMBER 16, 1929

(ONE DAY BEFORE)

Violet scooped scrambled eggs onto Philippe's plate and added a pair of biscuits. She poured him coffee. "When are you going to get out of that neighborhood like I said?"

Philippe, his mouth full of biscuit, mumbled something garbled, took a swallow of coffee, and tried again. "Skippy'll be back on Sunday. He'll take over for me for a while."

After last night's discussion with Gabe, she wanted to shake her brother and demand he tell her what else he was doing for Dolly White. She didn't like him sniffing around danger this way—but Gabe was right. He was a grown man. She settled for saying, "I don't like it."

"I know you don't. I'm not letting them drive me out. A man doesn't cut and run." Philippe yawned, and it made Violet yawn too. This was their usual routine. They closed the speak at five in the morning, cleaned up, and were locking the basement by six thirty. Philippe went off to do his rounds while Violet shopped for the day and did the books. Around one, when Philippe came home, they had breakfast and slept until midafternoon. Three days out of seven, Violet opened the hat shop for a few hours in the evening before opening the speak at ten. It was a topsy-turvy way to live, but she'd adjusted to it.

She crumbled her biscuit. "Laying low for a while isn't cutting and running."

"How can you tell the difference?"

"I thought Mama didn't raise any stupid children, but I guess I was—" She stopped as Philippe's head whipped around. A moment later something thumped against the door.

Philippe was out of his chair before she could push hers back. "It's not Gabriel," he said. "Hello?" He went to the door.

Violet followed, lifting the black tourmaline off the hook.

Philippe stood to one side and eased the door open. "Nobody." He looked down and stiffened. "Give me the stone."

"What is it?" She pressed the tourmaline into his hand.

He opened the door wider, and she stood on tiptoe to peer over his shoulder. A rectangular packet lay in front of the door. It was small but looked thick. She heard her brother breathe out and watched as he squatted. "There's blood," he said, sweeping the tourmaline over the surface of the package. He sniffed deeply. "Gabriel's." He dropped the stone and sprang up.

"Come back inside," she said.

"Stay here." He loped down the hallway.

"Philippe!"

He ignored her, pausing at the door to the outside stairs then disappearing through it. She pushed the door nearly closed and waited. A few minutes later, he came back. "Nobody I can see."

"They're long gone," she said. She didn't want to touch the package. She knew it wasn't cursed with blood magic, but her fingers turned cold at the thought of touching it.

Philippe picked it up and stepped across the threshold.

"You're not opening that on my table," Violet said.

He pushed his plate aside and picked up a kitchen knife. He slipped the tip of the knife under the flap. His fingers shook. He paused then dragged the knife across. The soft burr of the ripping paper filled the room. Philippe took the far end of the envelope and tipped it up.

Something slithered out onto the table. It was silvery, tipped with red: a gray braid. The darkening stain at the end looked daubed on, as if someone had dipped the tips in blood.

Philippe began panting, and she knew he was fighting to stay in human form. His grip clenched on the envelope. She reached over and tugged it from his fingers, pressed on the side to tent it open, and looked in.

"There's a note." She fished it out and unfolded it. The words were block printed in black ink.

The shape-shifter for the tattooist. 11:30 P.M., followed by an address.

"What is this?" she whispered.

"They have Gabriel."

"This is Dolly White's doing. She'd gotten you into something."

Philippe shook his head. "It's got nothing to do with her. This is about me—those men and me. They knew I was a shape-shifter."

"It started after you began working with her."

"It started before, Violet, with Farrell and the Doucette girl in the market."

"What's that's got to do with you?"

"I'm a shifter. They tried to force me to switch in a tony neighborhood. It would have caused a panic, and they would have shot me dead before I changed back."

"I know that."

"They can squeeze the Doucettes for being shifters, not for running shim. And then the territory's theirs."

"I still think this is about Dolly White. What are you doing for her?"

"An hour's work at the Earnshaw house, a bit of muscle, nothing more. It's not . . . this." He picked up the note. "Queen Anne Hill." He sucked in a deep breath and released it.

"I don't like this."

"I know my way around up there," he said.

"You're not going!"

"It's Gabriel."

"We'll get help. Tom, a couple of boys from the bar, your friends . . ."

"Don't you think they'll be expecting that?"

"You're not going," she said again, as if she could make it be true.

He stared. He was no longer on the verge of changing. He was calm. Sometimes, at odd moments, she looked at him and saw the man he was, not the younger brother she had always watched over. Now was one of those moments, and she hated it.

"If it were Pedro," he said, "would you go?"

"That's not fair," she said.

He started to turn, and she put her hand on his arm. "Wait. We've got time to plan. Come downstairs with me. We're going to call Dolly White right now."

"You think she'll help?"

"She damned well better."

~

Mid-morning, the party invitations arrived from the printer. Fiona and Dolly sat in the drawing room addressing them. Fiona wanted to be sure they all went out on the same day, as society matrons paid attention to such things.

After Lester's visit the previous day, Fiona had grown quiet. Dinner was an ordeal. Francis asked more and more pointed questions. Earnshaw commented once or twice about Commission business but mostly bent over his plate with all his attention on his food. Dolly managed to hold her own, but she didn't know what was troubling Fiona.

The girl seemed to have trouble concentrating. She kept sighing. Finally, she stood, startling Dolly, and headed for the door. "I'll be in the garden," she said.

Dolly set down her pen and the list. Was Fiona drinking or on shim again? There wasn't any sign of it. Had Rob Loughlin contacted her? Had he broken things off?

Dolly waited a minute or two then went out through the kitchen door to the cool fall garden, where Fiona sat in the pergola. Dolly went up the three steps and sat down across from her, hands folded in her lap, without speaking. The pergola, rarely used, was free of any earshot gems. It made a good place to talk.

Fiona was staring at the dark hedge, the boundary of the back garden. "I've been thinking about Henry," she said.

"The man in the car?"

Fiona nodded. "I think, what they did to Philippe, it must have been his idea. I think Henry must be up to something. I'm going to discuss it with Francis."

"Up to what?"

She looked at Dolly. "The wolf-woman in the market? What if Henry or one of the others forced her to transform with one of those lazuli charms? You said so yourself. I think Henry is ginning up fear of shape-shifters by creating . . . situations."

"What for, though? Does he just hate shape-shifters?"

Fiona rubbed her hands as if she were washing them. "I didn't say anything before, but when Uncle Mort was here, when he was arguing with Daddy, I recognized the name he mentioned. The Doucettes. They deal in shim."

"Most of Seattle knows that."

"There's a shim ring from the east side moving in, muscling them."

"How do you know this?"

"When you buy shim, you hear things." Fiona continued to fidget. "It's hard to prove the Doucettes have a criminal business. Rob used to tell me stories. The Doucettes are well protected and so are their criminal activities. The same way Violet is, I guess. The police take their money to ignore what's going on. But, if you turn people against them because they're shape-shifters, that's different. It's the Commission's business. If they're scrutinized for being wolves, if they're a danger . . . they'd be vulnerable to *that*, wouldn't they?"

Dolly looked at Fiona. *She's smart, although you wouldn't know it at first,* Marguerite had said. Dolly had met Fiona when she was deep in a shim haze. Since then she had assumed the girl was distracted by lovesickness and party planning, but Fiona had been paying more attention than Dolly had realized. Dolly had missed it. She was slipping.

"Yes, they would be, along with every other shape-shifter in the city," she said. "Do you think Henry is dealing shim? Is he challenging the Doucettes? That seems dangerous."

"I think he's helping someone else. I . . . I heard talk, sometimes."

"This is what you want to share with Francis? It's pretty thin, Fiona. You're basing this theory on the fact that Henry high-hatted you in the street."

"That's *not* the only reason. That street thug used a charm on Philippe—we both saw it. Did he look like he could afford a gold amulet? Someone with money is helping them. I'll bet Henry and some of his friends were in Pike Street Market when the wolf woman ran wild."

"Do you think Henry could embark on a plan like this without Francis knowing?"

"I do. Francis wouldn't allow such a thing. Underneath all the bluster, he's really a good man, Dolly."

Dolly twirled the end of her scarf.

Fiona's gaze followed her hand. "Oh, I *know* he's harsh with women. *I* warned *you*, remember? But he's not . . . He's fair. I'm sure he's fair."

Harsh with women. She made it sound as if Francis were a stern disciplinarian, sending disobedient girls to bed without supper. She waited until her heartbeat slowed. "I find it hard to believe Francis wouldn't know about something this elaborate. He's the leader of the Order."

"Francis wouldn't permit innocent people to be attacked. I can't believe that."

A picture of Sofia, frozen in ice, filled Dolly's mind. An innocent. And the owner of the simple silver locket, invisible, unnamed, unknown. An innocent. Usually, Dolly didn't give two shakes for "innocents," who were mostly just women too weak to protect themselves, but it galled her to hear Fiona using that word when she was talking about Francis.

She had broken the first rule of her business. She'd started to think of Fiona as a partner instead of a mark. Fiona had put all the pieces together, quite well, and resolutely looked away from the obvious conclusion. Dolly imagined the scene: Fiona carefully laying out the evidence for Francis, along the way revealing how much more Dolly knew about magic than she had let on. Francis was already wary; would he assume Dolly, unlike Fiona, *did* consider it likely the White King's crown prince would help a new ring of shim runners if it lined his own pockets?

She didn't think Francis would hurt his sister, but he would definitely raise his guard even more. Dolly needed him confident and careless right now.

Fiona had always been the weak link in the plan. Dolly had assumed the problem would be her love of drink and shim, not a sudden dive for the comfortable jail cell of misplaced family loyalty.

"You may be on to something," she said slowly. She was so close to wrapping everything up. If Fiona persisted, Dolly might have to take measures. Fiona might have to have a set-back. Dolly could arrange it easily if she had to, just a little something slipped into Fiona's evening coffee. The space be-hind her breastbone suddenly felt hollow. She wondered what was causing that. "I think you're going to need more proof before you speak to your brother, though. Do you think you could find out—"

Fiona looked past her. Dolly turned to see Inez coming across the grass.

"There is a telephone call for you, miss."

Dolly looked at Fiona, but the girl was looking at her.

"It's for you, Miss Dolly."

Dolly stared. "Me?"

Inez nodded. "A woman named Maureen. It's a question they have about your hat."

"Oh. Yes." She stood up. "The hat."

"Is everything all right?" Fiona came up behind her.

"Everything's fine. This will just take a moment."

She followed Inez back into the house. The earpiece of the elegant candlestick phone lay on the oak table. If Violet was calling the house, something had gone badly wrong. Was it Penske?

Dolly looked around. She sat down on the pink chair and spoke into the mouthpiece. "This is Dolly White."

There was a rush of air. Then Violet said, "Just what have you gotten my brother into?"

Dolly glanced behind her then tipped up the candlestick phone, checking its base, and ran her fingers quickly over the underside of the telephone table. No earshot gems; the call should be safe—Ambrose Earnshaw valued his own privacy too much for that.

"What?" she said.

"They took Gabe. They want Philippe."

"Who did? It's got nothing to do with me." Dolly heard Fiona talking to Inez as the girl walked back to the drawing room, and lowered her voice slightly. "I can't help you."

"You are going to help us," Violet said. "Somehow you're going to help us get Gabe back. Tonight."

"Not tonight," Dolly said. Her mind raced. Everything was in place, nearly. But she needed Philippe. Maybe she could hire someone else, but she never liked to do that at the last minute. Penske had agreed to the plan, but the transformation of Sofia had rattled him. She wasn't confident he could bring himself to carry the girl's body up to the house, not with the elemental sucking life out of him with every hour. All that business, loading Sofia into a car, unloading her . . . She needed backup, and there was no one else she could trust. She needed Philippe, and he was not in place.

"This is a bootlegger squabble, obviously," she said. "Don't try to involve me."

"It is not. You think I don't know how bootleggers think? They fight with cops and guns. Not this. This is all part of whatever's going on—that thing in the Pike Street Market, your Order of Saint Michael."

"It isn't *my* order," Dolly said, mainly to give herself time to think. She couldn't lose Philippe now, and she couldn't afford Violet as an enemy.

"You're in their house. You know what's going on, and you're pulling the strings on those rich white folks."

"It's not that easy." Her fingers twisted the cord between the earpiece and the candlestick, and she made herself stop. "All right. I'll meet you in an hour. I don't know what I can do to help, but I'll try."

"Come to the shop."

"No." She gave Violet the address of a small grocery at the bottom of Broadway Hill. Then she raised her voice slightly. "Very well, I'll call you in a day or two."

"You better be there," Violet said, and Dolly held a silent earpiece and listened to dead air.

She replaced it and pushed the chair gently back in against the table. This was a complication, not a setback. Not yet.

She went into the drawing room where Fiona sat, once more addressing envelopes. "I need to leave the house for a bit."

"You're going to go get your hat," Fiona said.

"No . . . the hat isn't ready. That was what they called to say."

"Dolly, I have more hats than a duck has feathers. I could give you one."

She laughed. "That's very generous, but don't you think I wanted to get my own hat? Something of my own?"

"I'm sorry. I didn't think."

"It's no matter. You are so very kind, but I do want to buy my own hat." She glanced at the doorway and sat down next to Fiona, lowered her voice to just above a whisper. "About that other matter. I think a little more . . . research might be needed before you talk to anyone."

"I wondered about that too," Fiona murmured. "If a certain person was in a... certain place when... that thing happened."

If Earnshaw was listening, a sentence so mangled and cryptic would certainly arouse his suspicions, but Dolly nodded and patted Fiona's hand. Leaning forward, she put her lips nearly against Fiona's ear and whispered, "Would Rob help you?"

"I—" Fiona drew away. Her face was flushed pink. She said in a normal tone of voice. "Ah, what color is your hat? If it's not a secret."

"Oh. Green."

"How perfect!"

"I have to go now," Dolly said.

"I'll have these done by the time you get back," Fiona said, gesturing.

Dolly smiled. "Bold words, Fiona. We'll see."

Mrs. Chambers sat at the kitchen table with two open cookbooks in front of her and a pad of paper. Dolly let the door shut behind her. "Mrs. Chambers, you said you needed salt, and I'm about to go to the grocery now."

The cook looked up and frowned at Dolly. "No," she said.

"No?"

Mrs. Chambers pulled over the notepad. "I'd never run out of salt, Dolly. It was baking powder. And I need dried currants for the biscuits tomorrow, and eggs. Here." She handed Dolly the list. "I usually count on Nick, but he's with the mister today."

"I'll just call a taxi," Dolly said. At least one thing was going right.

~

She shopped first. The small, neighborhood grocery was expensive compared to the Pike Street Market, but Dolly was spending Francis's money, so she didn't care. Carrying the shopping bag, she stepped out on the sidewalk. A dark-green convertible sat empty across the street. Fiddling with her cloche, she scanned the street.

"Here," Violet said, coming up on her right side. Philippe stood behind her.

"Let's get off the street," Dolly said. "Is there a place?"

"There's a square around the corner with a dry fountain and some benches," Philippe said. "This time of day, there's usually no one here. We won't stand out."

"Take us there."

The little square was not completely abandoned. An elderly man with a bag of peanuts was surrounded by a flock of iridescent gray pigeons. He didn't even look up as they sat down on the other side of the fountain.

"Tell me what happened," Dolly said, but before she even finished the sentence, Violet was speaking. She was quick and clear. When she was finished, Dolly shook her head.

"This has nothing to do with me," she said. "I can give you the name of a policeman who might help, but that's it."

"I've got police," Violet said. "Gabe'll be dead before they clear the door."

"Are you sure it isn't carnies?" Dolly said. "Or a collector? Plenty of unscrupulous people try to capture shape-shifters."

"Not their style," Philippe said. "A Mickey Finn for you to drink and a silver collar around your neck, that's how they do it."

"This is too organized, and it's right after that thing up on Broadway."

"Yes," Dolly said. "That was strange. Someone is trying to squeeze shape-shifters."

"It's about shim," Violet said. "They're after the Doucettes. And I know the neighborhood. I used to live there. There are several homes with greenhouses. When I—when we lived there, someone came to my husband to talk about buying shimmer from us."

"You grew shimmer?"

"Of *course* we did. The herb isn't illegal. Lots of people use it. It isn't until you poison it with blood magic and turn it into shim that it's dangerous. We didn't grow much, because you don't need much for rubs and salves. But someone on that street was growing a lot, and they wanted more. They *weren't* working for the Doucettes."

"How long ago was this?"

Philippe stirred. "Two years ago."

Dolly turned away and stared at the dry fountain.

Mortimer Lester had gone into the shim-running business a little over two years ago, if the ledger she'd stolen was accurate.

She needed it to seem like Francis had stolen the void mask Earnshaw kept in his vault, and with Sofia's body, she had more than enough to put him in the frame. Bringing down Lester wasn't necessary, although it would be satisfying. If she told Violet and Philippe about the ledger, she would be giving up leverage with no profit.

But Philippe could not help her if he surrendered himself to Lester.

The hollow feeling in her chest was back. Was she sick? She rarely got sick, but she couldn't remember having this sensation before.

She shouldn't be this confused. It was a simple calculation; she would not give away an advantage. She had never given away an advantage.

"You know something," Violet said. "I can see it."

"I'm thinking."

Dolly stood and walked over to the fountain. "I'm not quite like other people," she said.

"You don't know if you're human."

"I'm human," Dolly said.

Violet went on talking as if she hadn't heard. Her voice was low and even. "I can't care about whether you think you're human. That's your problem. I care about *this*. I already lost one man I loved. I'm not going to lose my brother, and we're not going to lose Gabe. I don't have time to wait while you decide if you have a heart. Are you going to help us or not?"

Dolly stared down into the dry, dusty bowl. There was nothing here to remind her of the Twilight Lands, quite the opposite, but her mind took her to the sky-blue waterfall, plunging down from overhead, to the lush, overgrown gardens and ruins, to the sounds of their singing, the ones who had found her. They helped her. They made her stronger. Their gifts made her good at what she did, but there was no denying they had changed her.

If Philippe had fallen into the Twilight Lands, Violet would never have stopped searching for him. The idea of a sister or a brother who would risk everything for her . . . that gave her a twinge of a feeling she thought might be envy.

She walked back over and sat down. "Philippe, where did you put the package I gave you?"

He put his hand to the small of his back. "It's safe," he said.

She nodded. "Violet, that's what you need. Tear out a couple of pages and offer them those. It's the leverage you need to get your tattooist back."

Speaking softly, she filled them in.

Chapter Ten

NOVEMBER 16, 1929

(ONE DAY BEFORE)

"**ALL THE INVITATIONS ARE** addressed," Fiona said. "They'll go out in the post tomorrow."

"Very good," Earnshaw said. He forked up some mashed potatoes.

"Francis isn't joining us tonight?" Dolly asked.

"The Order has a neighborhood needing help. Some families requested protection from wolves."

Dolly patted her lips with her napkin. "The Denny Regrade."

Earnshaw smiled. "No."

"There are so many neighborhoods in Seattle I still don't know."

"It's Queen Anne Hill that's having some trouble."

Fiona glanced at Dolly. "Are you staying in tonight, Daddy? You've been out almost every night this week."

"And, unfortunately, I'll be out tonight too. I'll spend the night at my club."

Fiona looked startled. "Is there something going on?"

Earnshaw stretched his legs and leaned back in the chair. He stroked his mustache. "Running the Commission is demanding work, Fiona, that's all."

"I know."

"I'm glad you know, because one day Tony will be on the Commission, and it will be a help to him to have an understanding wife."

Fiona took a bite of chicken. "I'll do my best, Daddy," she said.

~

"Do you want some tea?" Dolly said. She stood in the drawing room doorway.

"I don't think so." Fiona beckoned Dolly closer. When Dolly sat down next to her, she whispered, "I took your advice and sent that . . . message."

Dolly kept her voice to a murmur. "You're waiting, then?"

"I think if I do more . . . research? It'll be better." She spoke at normal volume. "Do you think squab Véronique will be too rich?"

"It's just right, a wise choice." Dolly stood. "I'm going to join Mrs. Chambers for tea in the kitchen."

"I'm going to bed," Fiona said.

On her way to the kitchen, Dolly fingered the small packet of herbs in her pocket. She only needed one more night, and Fiona was holding off on taking any foolish action.

It would be best to help her forget anyway. It would be the prudent approach.

Still, Dolly might come back to Seattle someday, and it would be good to have more helpers. She could hold off. She would focus on tonight.

She chatted with Mrs. Chambers while the cook drank her tea but didn't drink any herself. Tea sometimes made her jittery, and she couldn't risk shaky hands tonight.

~

Violet pulled up in front of the house in Queen Anne Hill just as her watch ticked past eleven. The drapes were drawn tightly, and only a thread of light leaked out. The porch light was off, but she could see two men standing in the pool of shadow there.

She stepped out of the car and walked across the street. The house had a low whitefence and a set of stepping-stones up to the porch. It was a newer style, a bungalow. She knew from memory that the yard, while narrow, reached back a long way, and most of it was probably taken up by a greenhouse. The sharply pitched roof was broken by a dormer window, dark right now.

"You can stop right there," the man on her left said as she opened the gate.

She didn't bother to look behind her, even though she had heard footsteps as soon as she'd gotten out. "Your gunsels can root through my car all they want. He's not coming. We have another deal to propose."

"There's no other deal. Bring the shape-shifter here, or say goodbye to your blind skin-sticker."

"You might want to check with your boss before you say that."

"Don't need to."

"You sure about that? I'm going to open my purse now." She snapped her bag open and drew out one of the pages from the ledger. "Show him this. I'll be waiting in the car. If he decides he wants to talk, flick the porch light twice."

He didn't reach for the paper. Violet stood, keeping her breath steady, glad to see her hands didn't shake. After several seconds, the man on the right stepped down and plucked it out of her hand. She turned without a word and made herself stroll back to the car. Her heart pounded as she slid into the driver's seat and shut the door. Without meaning to, she reached up and clutched the Virgin medallion hanging around her neck.

~

Light streamed out of the back windows, and the greenhouse glowed faintly in comparison, like a paper lantern. Philippe hopped the fence and dropped low to the ground. He wore dungarees and a jacket, no shirt, with his old hunting knife on a sheath around his neck.

He crawled forward, straining to hear, watching out of the corners of his eyes for any movement. The yard was empty. There was a danger that Lester would agree to Violet's proposal quickly, but there was no change in the activity of the house, at least none he could see or sense. Maybe Lester was still thinking it over.

He opened the greenhouse door. The smell of cinnamon and black pepper overwhelmed him, and he pressed his hand over his mouth to stifle a cough. Tables lined the long room, each one filled with shimmer seedlings in pots. He waited, listening. No one was in the greenhouse itself except him.

He crept forward, smelling old blood.

Close to the door into the house, a potting station held a glass knife, a mortar and pestle, and a quartz bowl. This was where they added the blood spells that converted shimmer into shimmer-shim. This wasn't just a greenhouse; it was a laboratory. The connecting door to the house was closed.

From the outside, the house looked much like the one Violet and Pedro had rented. The greenhouse probably opened into a mudroom, and from there into the pantry and kitchen of the house.

He knelt and pressed his ear against the door. At first, he heard nothing. Then he detected a faint rumbling, rising and falling. Voices.

He reached up and slowly turned the doorknob.

~

Dolly didn't try to sleep. She laid out her supplies carefully, put each one into her small cloth bag. She packed her handful of passports and all the cash she had but left her clothes hanging and her notions in place on the table. She lined up her shoes by the bed and sat down to wait.

Over the years, she had gotten good at waiting. That was, in some ways, what most jobs were about . . . waiting until the marks got greedy enough, sentimental enough, arrogant enough, or fearful enough to put aside their common sense, to ignore what their brains and their senses told them, what their so-called morals told them, and do the stupid thing. It was amazing how often they would.

Waiting gave her time to think, though, and tonight she didn't like that. She didn't like the loose ends floating out of her reach; Penske, as weak as he was, and Philippe, distracted.

She realized she was rubbing her hands together and made herself stop.

Dolly didn't get nervous, but she wondered if this was what

getting nervous felt like.

~

The knob turned and turned as the tongue drew back. Philippe opened the door and slid inside. He pushed it shut, gripping the knob so there was no click. The mudroom was dark. He took off his jacket, folded it, put it in the corner, and set his shoes on top of it.

He could hear a voice more clearly now. He'd thought there were two, but now there was only one, male. It wasn't Gabriel. The man was talking to someone.

Philippe wasn't ready to change yet, but he was close. He closed his eyes, opened his mouth wide, and let his tongue roll out, relying on the puma's sense of smell.

A man, an enemy, metal, carrion . . . and his mate. His mate was in that room.

He forced the puma's instincts into the background. Gabriel was in the room. Metal . . . The other man had a gun.

Gabe spoke. He sounded cheerful. "How's your nose?"

"Shut up, you." The other man's voice was nasal, muffled.

"Do you think I broke it?" Gabe said.

"I can *shut* you up."

"Sure you could, now. Both my hands are tied."

Oh, God, Gabriel, don't taunt him, Philippe thought.

It was a risk to change in the house, where they probably had magicked silver and other charms, but he was strongest when he was in his animal form. He unbuttoned his fly and slipped out of the dungarees.

~

Violet resisted the urge to look at her watch again. Twenty minutes had gone by, and the porch was still dark. She'd expected it to take a while but maybe not this long. By now, Philippe should be inside the house.

She thought about going up to the door and pounding on it, just to create a distraction. That wasn't the plan. She had to trust her brother.

Headlights appeared in the rearview. As she looked up, they winked out. The driver had turned them off.

Her heartbeat rattled her whole chest. She started the car. Leaving her own headlights dark, she pulled away from the curb. Lester had called for reinforcements.

Don't panic, she said to herself. This had always been a possibility. The car behind her was nearly invisible until it drove through the stream of light cast by a neighbor's lighted window. Violet made herself drive slowly away, taking the first right turn. She flipped on the headlights. It was a good thing she knew the neighborhood. She watched, but no one followed her.

Would Philippe know? Would he be able to get Gabriel to the second rendezvous point?

~

The puma crouched by the half-open door, ears flattened. He could tell from the sounds around him that there were more predators in the house now, enemies. His mate was in distress. And he was angry, because something constricted his movements; something tangled around his neck, carrion leather and metal. He didn't like it.

The first adversary came into view, his back to the puma.

He sprang. He knocked the man down. A piece of metal skidded across the floor. The man fought, but the puma got a good grip on a shoulder. Bone crunched. The man went limp but still breathed. The puma turned his head to get a better hold, to break the man's neck, when he heard his mate.

He stood, leaving his prey reluctantly, and padded to his mate's side. He put his head on his mate's leg and let a rumble of contentment spill out of him, closing his eyes.

His mate made a sound, the same sound, over and over, speaking, speaking a name, calling him back.

"Philippe."

He opened his eyes.

"Something's going on. Something bad. We need to get out of here."

Gabriel was tied to a chair. Philippe rocked back on the balls of his feet. He gasped when he saw Gabriel's face, swollen and covered with bruises.

"I'm okay," Gabriel said, "but we need to move."

Philippe pulled the knife out of the sheath hanging off his neck and cut the thin lines that bound Gabriel. His lover's knuckles were bruised. "How many came after you?" Philippe asked.

"Three, counting the driver."

Philippe snorted a laugh in spite of himself. Plainly, they didn't know Gabriel. "But they hurt you."

"Just a beating. It was you they wanted."

There was a crash in the other room, raised male voices.

He cut the cords around Gabriel's feet. The room smelled of blood. In the corner, next to the gun, lay a folded piece of twinkling fabric. Philippe stood. He bent down for the gun and recognized the fabric: magicked silver mesh.

"A silver net?"

Gabriel said, "They were going to force you to change, and . . ."

Philippe knew the rest. Trap the puma in silver, torment him, then release him in a public place, with lots of people. Another shape-shifter run wild—this time a colored man—with him dead at the end of it, and now an excuse for the Commission to step in.

"I don't have my cane," Gabriel said, gripping the arms of the chair. "Philippe, I haven't walked around without a cane in ten years. I don't know if I—"

"We have it in the car," he said.

"You do?"

"And you can lean on me until we get there."

Gabriel stood cautiously. "Someone came pounding on the door just now. I thought it was Violet, but—"

". . . who *is* she?" Philippe flinched as a man's voice roared the words from the other room.

"I remember that voice," Gabriel said. Philippe took Gabriel's arm. In the corner, the wounded man scrabbled at the floor, trying to pull himself to his feet. Philippe stopped, staring. He wondered if he should kill him, but he'd never killed a man before, and to do it coldly . . . He needed to get Gabriel out of here.

Furniture crashed. "Were you working together? What is she *after*?"

"I don't . . . *blackmailed* me . . ."

Philippe half dragged Gabriel into the mudroom.

"Stay away from the boss!" a third voice shouted, and a shot boomed though the house.

Gabriel stumbled once as they scrambled into the

greenhouse.

Behind him, shots exploded.

"Dear God," Gabriel murmured. He started forward and crashed into one of the tables, Pots tipped sideways and rolled off the table. Philippe didn't remember it being this cold outside. "I've got you." He guided Gabriel out to the fence. Only then did he stop. "Shit."

"What?"

"I forgot my clothes."

~

She went up the stairs silently, to the third floor. The green-and-gold carpet rubbed against her bare feet. The small bag bumped on her hip.

She walked past Earnshaw's workroom, with its gleaming, empty tables, down to the wall with the affinity lock.

She sat down cross-legged and breathed deeply.

~

Violet nosed her little car down the alley and waited. She couldn't see the house from here. She rolled her window halfway down. Her free hand found the medallion and rubbed it without her consciously willing it.

A popping sound carried to her, and then more, like a series of New Year's firecrackers. She caught her breath and nearly jumped out of the car. Those were shots. She reached for the door handle then made herself stop, made herself wait.

The street before her lit up as lights came on. She knew the neighborhood. No one would be in a rush to call the cops.

Rubber squealed on pavement.

Things got quiet.

She swallowed. Philippe? Gabriel?

One by one, lights went out.

She waited for sirens. She heard none.

~

Don't let your fingers tremble, she thought, but they did, the merest vibration, as she filled the bone needle with the blood from the preservation vial. Holding her breath, she inserted the tip under the spider silk bladders, filling each of the three flat sacs adhered to her right hand. For a moment, she enjoyed the novelty of her fear, but only a moment. This was a job; she needed to concentrate.

She waited for the space of four breaths, for Francis's blood to warm up from the heat of her fingers. Everything she'd read assured her this should work. It *should.* If it failed, she would know immediately from the blazing wall of pain that would surround her. While she didn't like pain, she could deal with it—failure was another matter. If it failed, if she lost the use of her hands, she'd transform from an independent agent to prey.

Stop, she thought. *This will work.* She forced herself to calmness. When her heartbeat was slow and even, her fingers steady, she pressed them into the blue-jeweled indentations of the hand shape on the affinity vault's lock.

~

Violet couldn't stand it any longer and started to get out of the car when the block of light at the intersection picked out a halo of silver. A shadow, no, two shadows, joined, moving toward her.

She jumped out, ran around, and opened the door. Gabriel was gasping for breath, holding his midsection like someone who'd taken a beating. Her brother was nearly invisible next to him.

"Hurry!" Now she could hear sirens, distant but growing closer.

Gabriel grunted as he clambered into the back. Philippe slid in next to him.

She ran back around and climbed in behind the wheel. The car started, and she reversed, backing all the way out of the alley as the wail of the sirens grew.

"We have to get home. We need to take care of Gabe. I told Miss White I'd help her, and I need to be there before one. And I need pants."

"Are you *naked*?"

"I forgot my clothes," Philippe said.

She shook her head and turned right. "I can't go anywhere with you," she said.

~

NOVEMBER 17, 1929

She came into the study, locking the door behind her. It was a little after one in the morning. The left pocket of her skirt hung heavy. She had already left her valise in the foyer closet.

Moving carefully in the dark, she approached the French

doors, pausing only to toss a small, velvet-lined case into the shadows underneath Earnshaw's desk.

The counterspell took fifteen minutes, if everything went perfectly. But it didn't go perfectly. The nerve tenderness in her thumb and finger made the gestures more difficult.

She was only a third of the way into it when a key rattled faintly in the front door. She stopped, her heart beating high in her throat. The front door opened. What if it was Earnshaw, changing his plans? Then what?

The door slammed, and someone crossed the foyer with quick strides. It was Francis. At least now she knew where he was. She cleared her mind of distraction and began again.

She hoped the others were in place.

The spell was agonizing, but finally she spoke the final couplet and made the final pass. She was reaching for the handles of the French doors when the doorknob rattled behind her, and a key clicked in the lock.

"I want that ledger," Francis said, throwing open the door. "Lester's accounts. It's not in your room. Where is it?"

Her fingers touched the handle. He ran toward her, grabbed her by her hair, and pulled her away before she could open it. "Oh, no you don't," he said. "Where is it?"

She didn't struggle. "You went into my room? Not very gentlemanly."

"You're no lady, Dolly. Or whatever your name is." His face was bright, eyes gleaming, not with anger but with glee. "Won't Dad be surprised, when he finds out he's not such a great *judge* of *character*?"

"Will he be surprised at your detailed *record keeping* of the waterfront magickers you've been shaking down?" she said. "Or disappointed in you for keeping incriminating evidence?"

His face darkened. "My notebook? Give it to me!"

"It's safe. You'll have it back when I'm sure I'm safe."

"No. You'll get it now. You'll get them both now. Then we'll talk about what you'll do to stay out of jail."

She lowered her eyes, hoping he would think she was being docile.

He went on. "Lester. Stupid fool told me *everything*! I should have known, when my buddy saw you walking with Loughlin downtown. You've been in cahoots with him the whole time, haven't you?"

"Loughlin? Fiona's beau?" She fanned herself with her hand. "Just let me open the door, Francis, please. It's so hot in here." She turned and reached for the handle.

He dragged her back again, hard against him, and slapped his forearm down across her throat. Pain bloomed from the pressure on the bruises. She tugged on his elbow. He smelled of blood and gunpowder. Gunpowder? She hadn't thought he'd go so far as to hurt one of his father's friends. Had he killed Lester himself?

"Where is my *notebook*?"

She observed her own struggles remotely. When her tugging and kicking grew weakest, she raised her hand in surrender.

Francis loosened his grip. Her knees gave way. He let her fall, still holding on to her hair.

"Fiona's room," she whispered.

He released her hair, and she fell against the door. Using the handle, she levered herself up, unlatching it. Francis had already wheeled away from her, his mind on the notebook.

Dolly pulled her sock doll from her pocket, looped the ribboned skirt around her hand, spun, and sapped Francis behind the ear. She was weak. Even though the doll's body was filled with sand and lead clay, he didn't fall. Black spots danced in her vision as she hit him again. She hit him once more. Francis dropped as if he had no bones.

Philippe came in through the door. "I thought he'd kill you, miss," he said. "I almost broke the door in."

"I'm glad you didn't." The spots faded. She pushed the French doors wide open.

"What took you so long?" Penske asked. He knelt on the flagstone walkway, the body of his niece cradled in his arms.

Dolly cleared her throat and felt a bolt of pain. "Philippe?" She went forward and bent down to help. Dizziness broke around her like a wave, and she staggered.

Penske struggled to stand, still holding his niece. Dolly knelt on the flagstones, taking the body and supporting it. Philippe offered Penske a hand, and the greengrocer pulled himself up. After a moment filled with the rasp of his breathing, he reached down and lifted Sofia's body upright. Dolly stood, put her arm around the dead girl's waist, and helped Penske carry her inside.

They arranged the girl, now wearing Dolly's gray suit and Dolly's face, on the sofa.

Penske lifted Sofia's hand, holding out the Saint Michael medallion.

"No." Dolly plucked it out of his hand.

"But she—"

"The family's already noticed it's missing." She slipped the Saint Michael the Protector medallion into the pocket of the gray skirt Sofia wore.

Philippe knelt by Francis. "You got him good, miss."

"Very few things bother me," she said, "but trying to kill me is one of them. It makes me mad."

"Are you well enough?" Penske asked. There was a light in his gaze she didn't trust. "That vault, it's dangerous. I could help you."

"I'll manage," she said. There was no point in telling him she'd already opened the vault.

He reached down and pressed his hand lightly against the dead girl's cheek. As he turned away, he saw the case she'd dropped. With a soft exclamation, he started toward it.

"Let's just leave that where it is, Mr. Penske," she said.

He frowned, shrugged, and tucked his hands into his trouser pockets.

"This one had a busy night," Philippe said, looking down at Francis. "I think he killed some men at the Queen Anne Hill house." The expression on his face wasn't anger. It was determination.

"How is your tattooist?" She joined him, staring down at the unconscious lump.

"He'll be all right."

Helping them had been a good choice, the right choice, it turned out. Maybe she would want to work in Seattle again sometime, and the three of them could be useful

She nodded down at Francis. "Well. I think Volunteer Park is a good place for him."

She turned to Penske. "An hour before sunrise, you tip the police," she said. "And you ask for the name I gave you."

"Robert Loughlin."

She nodded. "Are we square?"

"Square," he said.

~

NEAR DAWN, NOVEMBER 17, 1929

The cabbie waited, persuaded by the promise of a sawbuck. Dolly knocked on the door twice, once, then twice more.

Violet opened the door herself. She led Dolly to the back of the shop and down the stairs. Philippe pushed a mop across the wood floor. He grinned at Dolly.

"It go well?" Violet said.

"Quite." Dolly pulled the envelope with the jewelry out of her bag. "When the trial's over, give Fiona these, please."

"You're leaving with her thinking you dead?"

"I want every tearstain, every tremble in her voice on the witness stand, to be real. Once he's gone away, you can let her know."

"That's coldblooded."

Dolly shrugged.

"It might not go to a trial, you know."

"You mean, the White King might step in? Send Francis to an asylum?"

"Wouldn't be the first time."

"If that happens, give her these anyway."

Violet looked at her.

"She'll be fine." Dolly didn't really know why she was still discussing this. "She has her man, they have the evidence, and she'll have the jewels."

"You take chances, miss," Philippe said. He sounded admiring. Violet tossed him a look then glanced back at Dolly.

"She know you framed her brother?" Her tone was curious, not censorious.

"I didn't, exactly." Dolly pulled folded bills, half of Francis's cache, out of her bag. "He did kill a woman. It just wasn't me."

Violet said, "Not just women."

Dolly held out the money.

Violet did not reach for it. "You already paid us."

"You earned it."

Violet took the folded bills. "You want the ledger back?"

"No need."

"I think Lester's ring is as dead as he is, anyway."

"They'll never pin Lester's murder on Francis," Philippe said. "And Mr. Earnshaw may see his son go to jail, but he doesn't lose anything."

Violet looked narrow-eyed at Dolly. "Why are you smiling?"

"Ambrose Earnshaw may lose something," she said, "Like his precious commission. He had a lot of things in his safe, including a shifter-stone amulet. It was one of a set of two, in a case. The other one was missing."

"Nobody'll ever know that," Philippe said. Then he gasped. "You told Penske to leave it there! Was that—"

Dolly shrugged. "He may have some awkward questions at his next meeting."

"Well." Violet put the money in the till. "It's been an adventure working with you, Dolly."

"Not Dolly anymore."

Violet raised her eyebrows. "So who're you going to be, then?"

She thought of the passports in her bag. Dolly White's was where she had left it, in the desk in Earnshaw's study, and Dolly White was dead. Dorothy Whitson, Blanche Borden, Vivienne Underhill, Comeuppance Rather . . . the name she was christened with, the name she hadn't used in many, many years.

She thought of the mask in her bag. She remembered its silken touch on her face and the tiny claws. It was a powerful tool, able to impart a full-body illusion. Her client in Wichita might very well believe she'd been killed, murdered in Seattle. With the mask, she would be even more effective. It would be the best way to leave Dolly White behind forever.

She thought back to the ease with which she had changed her shape, one self dissolving into another, nearly erased... the way a little girl in a tenement basement had been nearly erased by her sisters, locked in a closet with a rotting floor. Her chest hollowed out again, the feeling she wasn't ready to acknowledge. Since San Francisco, those feelings had been sweeping over her without warning. She didn't like it.

She blinked. Violet was staring at her. "Well? Who?"

She smiled at Violet. "There are so many choices," she said, "and it's much too early to tell."

Epilogue

NOVEMBER 22, 1929

WICHITA, KANSAS

SHE SAT ON A bench in the terminal, waiting for her train, in a dark-red traveling suit—a shade of which Marguerite would have approved—and a red cloche. The suit was nowhere near as high quality as the one she had sold and nothing like the clothes she could buy in New York, but it was the best Wichita offered, and she liked it just fine.

Her valise sat at her feet. The space underneath the false bottom was stuffed with cash, what remained after she had sent off a bonus payment to her associate Meritage in San Diego, shipped a cash gift to Marguerite, and wired the rest of her payday into an existing bank account in New York City.

New York was a place where terrible things happened—some of them had happened to her—but it was also the place where you could make the biggest scores, if you were willing to take a risk, and she always was.

She'd sent a letter to her friend Mr. Friedman in Washington, DC, suggesting he read Dolly White's two-sentence obituary in the *Star-Invocation*. The army's Signal Intelligence Service should be as pleased with the notice as she was.

It had chafed her pride to put out the word her San Francisco grift failed, when the real scheme, to keep a powerful grimoire out of the hands of German wizard, had worked like magic.

Dolly, you can be proud of the work you've done, Friedman had said to her, at a meeting so private, it had never happened. And she'd said, *I'll be even prouder when your check clears, Mr. Friedman.* It didn't do to let those government men get above themselves.

She closed her eyes and let herself smile. Once she had delivered the void mask to her client and collected her pay, she'd treated herself to a suite in Wichita's most luxurious hotel. She'd gone to the central library and asked for recent copies of the *Seattle Star-Invocation* and the *Seattle Times.* The *Star-Invocation,* an Earnshaw champion, had settled for, "Tragedy in the Earnshaw house." The *Times* trumpeted, "Thieves fall out; society scion arrested for theft and murder." The Earnshaw case still held the front pages. Both newspapers reported that Francis Earnshaw had been working with the unnamed woman who had gone by the alias Dolly White, planning to rob his father's vault. Francis had murdered the woman in an argument. A local police officer accused the junior Earnshaw of extorting money from unlicensed magickers and involvement in the case of an unsolved fire on the waterfront two years earlier in which a botanical magician had died. He provided a notebook with dates and payments, and already several magickers and herbalists had come forward to give evidence.

Ambrose Earnshaw had stepped down as Commissioner of Magi and was taking an indefinite leave of absence.

She didn't think he had the will or the wherewithal to send his son to a private asylum somewhere, not now.

Mortimer Lester and three other men had been found dead in a house on Queen Anne Hill, a house Lester owned. The police were continuing to investigate.

None of the articles mentioned Fiona.

She wondered how the girl was doing. Did the girl have her jewels and her man? Maybe she'd write Violet a letter and ask. The thought made her frown. Fiona was a mark. You didn't write letters to see how a mark was doing.

"Miss Rather? Comeuppance Rather?" A uniformed porter approached her.

"Yes, that's me."

"I'm here to take you to your Pullman, Miss Rather. Shall I get your trunks? Your luggage?"

She stood up and stooped to pick up her bag. "Just this. And I'll carry it."

"Very well, miss."

The young porter led her into the opulent car. Many of the Pullman cars rolled empty since last month's stock market crash. She could afford one. And she wanted it.

"Would you like a lemonade, miss?"

"No, thank you." She tipped him a dollar, and his eyes widened. When he was gone, she sank into one of the velvet chairs, stretched her legs, and sighed.

She'd been many places, but somehow she always came back to New York. In two days she would be there, in the Big Apple. And there would be so many opportunities there for a girl like her.

Acknowledgments

TK

About the Author

MARION DEEDS was born in Santa Barbara, California, and moved to northern California when she was five. She loves the redwoods, the ocean, dogs, and crows.

She's fascinated by the unexplained, and curious about power: who has it, who gets it, what is the best way to wield it. These questions inform her stories.

Deeds has published *Aluminum Leaves* and *Copper Road* from Falstaff Books, with short works in *PodCastle* and several anthologies. She reviews fiction and writes a column for the review site *Fantasy Literature*.